S0-AHR-522

"I'm so scared. Please help me."

"Tell me where you are, honey, and I'll come get you. What do you see?"

"I don't know. They're keeping me locked in a room. I managed to sneak out and find a phone but I'm scared. I don't know where I am, Abby."

Abby looked to Luke, feeling helpless to do anything for her. "Try to find a window. Look out and tell me what you see."

"I don't know. I can't–"

Kenzie's scream pierced the air as sounds of a struggle ensued.

"Kenzie!" She reached out for Luke and he wrapped his arm around her. Heavy breathing filled the line. "Who is this? Why did you take her?"

Instead of answering, the person hung up.

Luke pulled Abby into his embrace. As he did, she felt his heart pounding as well. "This is good," he assured her. "At least we know she's still alive."

Abby nodded. He was right. She had to focus on that.

Kenzie was alive...at least for now.

Virginia Vaughan is a born-and-raised Mississippi girl. She is blessed to come from a large Southern family, and her fondest memories include listening to stories recounted around the dinner table. She was a lover of books from a young age, devouring tales of romance, danger and love. She soon started writing them herself. You can connect with Virginia through her website, virginiavaughanonline.com, or through the publisher.

Books by Virginia Vaughan

Love Inspired Suspense

Cowboy Protectors

Kidnapped in Texas

Cowboy Lawmen

Texas Twin Abduction
Texas Holiday Hideout
Texas Target Standoff
Texas Baby Cover-Up
Texas Killer Connection
Texas Buried Secrets

Covert Operatives

Cold Case Cover-Up
Deadly Christmas Duty
Risky Return
Killer Insight

Visit the Author Profile page at LoveInspired.com.

KIDNAPPED IN TEXAS

VIRGINIA VAUGHAN

LOVE INSPIRED SUSPENSE
INSPIRATIONAL ROMANCE

If you purchased this book without a cover you should be aware that this book is stolen property. It was reported as "unsold and destroyed" to the publisher, and neither the author nor the publisher has received any payment for this "stripped book."

LOVE INSPIRED® SUSPENSE

INSPIRATIONAL ROMANCE

ISBN-13: 978-1-335-58825-8

Kidnapped in Texas

Copyright © 2023 by Virginia Vaughan

Recycling programs for this product may not exist in your area.

All rights reserved. No part of this book may be used or reproduced in any manner whatsoever without written permission except in the case of brief quotations embodied in critical articles and reviews.

This is a work of fiction. Names, characters, places and incidents are either the product of the author's imagination or are used fictitiously. Any resemblance to actual persons, living or dead, businesses, companies, events or locales is entirely coincidental.

For questions and comments about the quality of this book, please contact us at CustomerService@Harlequin.com.

Love Inspired
22 Adelaide St. West, 41st Floor
Toronto, Ontario M5H 4E3, Canada
www.LoveInspired.com

Printed in U.S.A.

Put on the whole armour of God, that ye may be able to stand against the wiles of the devil.
—*Ephesians* 6:11

To Izzy, my sweet grandbaby. You light up my life.

ONE

Abby Mitchell crossed the street to drop a letter into the mailbox. It had been a long day and she was looking forward to spending the evening with her niece and nephew and maybe watching a movie or vegging out on the sofa.

Kenzie was waiting for her now across the street at the café. Abby had promised the fourteen-year-old a cookie crumble Frappuccino before they headed home.

A scream pierced the air.

Abby spun around and her heart failed. A man had Kenzie, his arms wrapped around her, trying to shove her into the back seat of his car.

"No!" Abby darted across the street and attacked the abductor, punching at his arms, kicking and screaming, anything to get him to release her niece.

The man spun around and elbowed her in the face, sending her tumbling backward to the street. Her elbows scraped the concrete and stung, but that pain was nothing compared to the feeling of watching him shove Kenzie into the back of his car. He slammed the door, jumped into the driver's seat, then sped away before she could even scramble to her feet.

"Kenzie!" She reached out her hand in a fruitless gesture as the car sped away. Kenzie stared at her through the back window, her young face frightened and begging for help.

A man rushed to where Abby still lay on the ground. "Ma'am, are you okay? Do you need help?"

She shook her head, eyes still glued to the car speeding away. "He took her. He took Kenzie."

"I'm going after him. Call 9-1-1," the man said before heading toward an SUV.

Abby scrambled to her feet. She couldn't let this man get in his car and leave without her. She needed to be there if—when—he tracked down Kenzie. Her niece would need *her*, not some stranger. She rushed to the SUV and pulled open the passenger's door. She didn't even realize who her rescuer was until she climbed into the passenger seat.

Her breath caught in her chest.

Luke Harmon. Her old boyfriend. "You," she said.

He started the engine of the car and glanced her way as he nodded. "Me."

Okay, then. Him. So be it. Abby slammed the door shut and pulled on her seat belt as Luke shoved the vehicle into Drive and took off after the silver sedan.

She clutched her shoulder, only now realizing how hard she'd slammed it against the pavement when the abductor shoved her. It hurt almost as much as her cheek where he'd elbowed her, but neither of those injuries was anything compared to the pain of seeing Kenzie staring at her through the back of the window, her eyes wide and full of fear.

"Call Caleb," Luke said, and the phone on the dash lit up at his voice recognition. "My cousin is now the chief of police," he explained. She knew who Caleb was. She lived here in their hometown of Jessup, Texas, while Luke had moved away years earlier and, she'd heard, joined the FBI.

A moment later, a man's voice answered.

"Luke, I can't talk now. I just got word of an abduction downtown."

"I know. That's why I'm calling. I saw it all. He got away with a teenage girl and we're in pursuit. Her mother's here with me."

"I'm sending backup to you right now. Where are you?"

"Heading east on Delaware, just passing Lexington."

Luke pressed the accelerator and sped up, closing the gap between them and the silver sedan. Abby's heart jumped in her chest. They were going to catch up to them!

"That's them," she cried.

Suddenly, another vehicle shot through the intersection and cut them off, horn blaring. Luke jerked the SUV to the right to keep from smashing into the car but lost control.

Abby screamed as the SUV jumped the curb and crashed into a tree. The airbag deployed and the force of the impact sent Abby straight into it, then back again as the seat belt caught. Her head slammed against the seat and the world seemed to spin for a moment.

Tears pressed against her eyes as she caught a glimpse of the sedan speeding away with Kenzie inside just as she lost consciousness.

* * *

"What's happening?" Caleb's voice shouted through the cell phone. "Luke! Luke, what was that noise?"

Luke's ears were still ringing from the impact. He pushed the airbag away as he struggled to find his bearings.

All he knew was that he'd failed. Again.

He managed to feel for the door handle and open it, tumbling out. The front end of his SUV was a tangled mess against the big oak tree.

Abby!

He stumbled around to the passenger-side door and pried it open. Abby was still in the seat but her head hung to the side. He checked her pulse. She was alive, just unconscious.

"Luke, what's going on?" Caleb's tone had turned frantic and Luke knew, if he could, his cousin would have crawled through the cell phone to reach him.

"We crashed. My passenger is unconscious. We need an ambulance."

"I've already got a team on the way. Are you okay?"

"Yeah, but the kidnappers got away. You're going to need to issue a BOLO on a four-door silver sedan."

"Already done."

He turned back to Abby and touched her face, gently tapping her cheek to try to wake her. He sighed in relief when, after a moment, she started moving.

He couldn't believe she was here. That it was really her. The woman he'd loved as a teenager. The woman he'd hoped to spend his life with. The woman who'd stomped all over his heart. Now that the immediate adrenaline rush had passed and the weight of the situation sank in, all the strength seemed to drain from his knees. He sat on the runner of the SUV to catch his breath.

He glanced down the road. The silver car was out of sight. It was gone and so was Abby's daughter.

Another car door slammed. Luke got up and looked around to see the driver of the other car heading his way like a bull on a mission. "What were you doing?" he shouted at Luke. "You nearly killed me."

"You should learn to watch where you're going," Luke responded.

He heard movement behind him and saw Abby tumbling out of the car. She ran toward him. "Where did they go?" His heart broke at the anxiousness on her face.

"I'm sorry, but they got away."

"No!" He caught her as her knees buckled and sobs racked her body.

All he could do was hold her as the ambulance wailed in the distance, matching her cries of anguish.

Within minutes, police were surrounding the area where Luke had smashed his SUV. The driver of the other vehicle calmed down and stopped shouting once he realized what had happened.

Abby sat in the back of the ambulance and tried to hold it together. The image of Kenzie's face, so pale and frightened, wouldn't leave her. Where was the girl now and what was happening to her? Abby didn't know, and each moment she didn't, it shattered her.

She pulled out her cell phone, surprised to find it still worked after the crash. She needed to call her neighbor. Someone needed to be there when her nephew, Dustin, came home from soccer practice. She didn't want the twelve-year-old to find out about Kenzie without someone there to help him through it. He'd already been deprived of so much over the past years.

Abby did all she could to keep from breaking down as she explained briefly to Janet what had happened. Her longtime neighbor promised to take care of Dustin and make sure he was okay until she got home. "Keep us informed," Janet said. "We will be praying for you and for Kenzie."

Abby thanked her, then leaned back on the ambulance gurney. Her head was still spinning and fear was pulsing through her. But as she pushed past her fear and worry about Kenzie, her eyes locked on Luke Harmon as he stood several feet from the ambulance.

He looked good. He'd filled out nicely since college, and his dark hair, hint of a stubble and those broad shoulders could be distracting. He always had been nice-looking.

And now he was back in town.

The last time she'd seen Luke had been the day they'd broken up. No… She closed her eyes, replaying the memory in her mind… the day she'd broken up with him. The look of pain that had been on his face had haunted her for years. But it had to be done. She'd had no choice. At least, that was what she'd told herself back then. Now she knew she'd been scared and foolish, a dumb kid making bad choices that hurt people—that definitely hurt Luke. And yet now his baby blue eyes stared at her, worrying over her well-being. She'd deceived him in the worst possible way and he'd still been there for her when Kenzie had been attacked. How was that even possible?

Of course, she knew all things were possible with God. That was something she'd come to realize over the last two years. Ever since her sister and her brother-in-law were killed in a car wreck and she'd taken on the responsibility of raising Kenzie and her brother, Dustin. She would never have made it through without her newfound faith in Jesus.

The paramedics transported her to the hospital, where doctors poked and prodded and wanted to do a CT scan. She refused it. She was feeling better, other than the dull ache of her cheek, and even that was nothing compared to the heart-wrenching panic at not knowing what had happened to Kenzie. Luke appeared in the hospital room's doorway. A man she recognized as the chief of police stood beside him. Caleb. She'd forgotten Caleb was Luke's cousin.

She jumped off the hospital bed, grabbing hold of the edge as her knees threatened to buckle again. "Did you find her? Did you find Kenzie?"

She saw by the look on both their faces that the answer was no.

"We're doing everything we can," Luke assured her. "Caleb has put out a BOLO for the car and for the driver's description. He's also issued an Amber Alert."

Caleb stepped forward and took out his notepad. "We're doing everything we can to find her, but I need you to tell me exactly what happened."

Abby thought back. "Kenzie wanted to go into the café. I told her we would go after I went to the mailbox. She was supposed to wait for me there on the sidewalk. Then I heard her scream and turned and saw that man grab her and push her into his car. I tried to stop him but I couldn't." Her voice cracked as she recounted the events. She choked back that emotion. Falling apart wouldn't help find Kenzie.

Luke folded his arms as she told her tale. He had come up to her so soon after it happened that he had to have seen the attack. She looked up at him. "Did you see the man?"

He shook his head. "I didn't get a good look at him. I was leaving the lawyer's office when I heard her scream and that's when I rushed over. You were already on the ground by the time I got there."

Caleb looked at Abby. "Did you recognize the man? Had you seen him before?"

She tried to think back but the man's face was a blur. An unfamiliar blur. "I don't think so. He didn't look familiar to me."

"What about Kenzie? Did she seem to know him?"

Abby shook her head. "No. He was older. I did see that. Probably early twenties. Kenzie would have no reason to know anyone like that."

She saw Luke's face twist. She'd heard he was FBI now and was probably thinking she had no idea what fourteen-year-old girls might do. But he didn't know Kenzie. He didn't know all she'd been through in the last two years.

"We're gonna need to set up some kind of trace on your phone," Caleb told her. "In case there's a ransom call."

She shuddered at the word *ransom*. She had a little savings but not much. Nothing that would entice a kidnapper. But she was willing to do whatever it took to get Kenzie back. Even if it meant cleaning out her life savings or borrowing against the house.

"Whatever it takes," she told him, and she meant it.

"We will also need to go through Kenzie's bedroom, pull her cell phone records and examine her computer. Would that be all right?"

Abby nodded. She would let them do whatever it took to find Kenzie. "Whatever you need. Please find her."

Oh, God, please keep Kenzie safe.

Luke stepped out of the room so Caleb could ask Abby some more questions about the abduction and about Kenzie in general. He walked into the hallway and closed the door behind him, but he wasn't going far. He leaned against the wall to catch his breath as the impact of the afternoon's events caught up to him.

Abby Mitchell.

Imagine running into her again.

It had been fifteen years since he'd seen her. Back then, she'd been so determined to get out of Jessup that he'd been sure she would never come back. It had never crossed his mind that returning to their hometown would mean bumping into her.

The heartbreak he'd endured had healed, but he'd still felt the sting when he'd looked into her lovely brown eyes. What really hurt was the not knowing why. She'd ended their relationship without ever giving him a reason. One moment, everything had been fine. The next, she was gone. He was man enough to admit that he'd harbored some resentment toward her for the way she'd treated him. However, as he glanced through the window on the hospital door and saw her looking so despondent, he couldn't help but feel a tug of sympathy for her.

Her daughter had just been kidnapped and he had the skills to help her get her back. Their past didn't matter. It couldn't. Her daughter was an innocent child, and he certainly couldn't hold her mother's behavior against the girl, especially when she might be in a lot of danger.

But just the girl's existence opened up another old wound for Luke. For Abby to have a teenage daughter, she would have had to jump right into another relationship, or—he grimaced at the other alternative—she'd left him so abruptly because she'd already found someone else.

The door opened and Caleb stepped into the hallway. "Abby's ready to go home. She said she would take you to the house and let you go through Kenzie's things. I'll send an officer over there to meet you and retrieve her electronics so we can start with the tech search now. The sooner we get on top of this, the better chance we have of finding the girl." Caleb knew their history. He'd been around back in the day, so his hesitation wasn't surprising. "I know you're not officially on the job, but I sure could use your help on this one, Luke. We don't get many kidnappings around here, so your expertise would be useful. Are you going to be able to handle this?"

He tensed. The last case he'd worked before coming to Jessup had been an abduction case. A nineteen-year-old woman had gone missing, one of six in the past three years who'd been kidnapped and murdered by a serial killer named Jack Shelton. They'd rescued her, but the case had gone downhill fast and Luke had lost one of his agents during the final confrontation with Shelton. He was currently on nonactive duty with the agency pending a hearing to either clear him or end his career with the FBI.

That case had gone wrong, but, he had to keep reminding himself, it was only one of a string of cases he'd worked during his career. He couldn't allow it to define him—and he couldn't allow his regrets to keep him from helping Kenzie. "Absolutely. The past is the past, right?" He said it with more confidence than he felt. It wouldn't be easy for his head or his heart to work closely with Abby, but it would be worth it if they ended up getting her daughter home safely.

Caleb pulled out his cell phone. "I'm heading back to the office to lead this from there. I'll do the paperwork to make your involvement official in case this goes to trial." He pushed his keys into Luke's hand. "Take my car. I'll catch a ride. Whenever you get back there, you can use one of the ranch's trucks while you're in town."

He walked off and Luke stepped back into the hospital room.

"Are you sure you shouldn't stay here longer?" Luke asked as Abby pulled on her jacket. "You were just in a car wreck where you lost consciousness. I'm surprised the doctors didn't want to keep you overnight."

She shrugged off his concern. "They did, but I need to get home. I need to be there for Dustin. He's only twelve years old and he's already lost so much. I'm all he has left."

That was enough of a reason for him. He helped her to the car, then turned to Abby for directions. "Where to?"

"You remember my parents' house? I live there now."

That she was back in town at all, much less with kids, was already shocking, but that she'd moved into her parents' old house was an even bigger surprise. She'd fought so hard to get out.

"Are your parents still living?"

"Mom died of kidney disease ten years ago. Danielle and Matt moved in to take care of Dad. When he died, they kept the house."

Okay, so that didn't really explain what *she* was doing there instead of her sister and brother-in-law. He shot her another glance. "So how did you end up with it?"

"Danielle and Matt were both killed in a car accident two years ago. As their only living relative, I became Kenzie and Dustin's guardian. I thought it was better not to uproot them, so I moved back to Jessup."

"So Kenzie isn't your daughter?"

Her eyes widened in surprise. "Why would you think that?"

"I just assumed. Although, I did find it odd that you were a mom," he said. "The Abby Mitchell I knew was all about her career. The last time I heard anything about you, you were working toward becoming an anchor at a national TV station."

Her body seemed to relax and she blew out a breath and nodded. "Yes, that's true. I was with a station in Atlanta when Danielle died. I gave that up to come here. Now I do the morning news on the local broadcast."

"That's quite a step down."

"I wish I could say it was an easy decision. It wasn't—but I know it was the *right* decision. I had to do what was best for the kids."

He did his best to hide his surprise. Abby Mitchell making the hard sacrifice for family? That was quite a change from the girl he'd known. "I'm sorry about Danielle. I know you two were always close."

"Thank you. Yes, we were."

Now it was her turn to question him. "I didn't know that you were back in town though. When did that happen?"

"I'm not. At least, not permanently. My grandfather died, and he left me and my cousins equal shares of his ranch. I'm just in town to settle the inheritance." Like Abby, he couldn't have gotten out of his hometown fast enough. Not much could have persuaded him to come back either, but he had to deal with settling his part of the inheritance. His cousin Caleb already lived in town, but his other cousins, Brett and Tucker, were supposed to be returning as well to settle the matter. He was hoping one or more of them would be willing to buy out his share.

"I'm sorry about your grandfather. Will you stay on at his ranch?"

"No." She knew better than anyone that the place didn't hold good memories for him, not after the nightmare his childhood had been, being used as a pawn between his mother and grandfather in their battle for control of Luke's life.

"A lot of things can change from when we were kids. My life certainly has."

That was true, but he doubted his perspective on his relationship with his grandfather would ever shift. No way could he forgive the old man for decades of making Luke's mother scrimp and struggle to pay the bills while Chet Harmon hoarded his wealth. When Luke's father had died, his grandfather had grown cold and distant, yet he'd still wanted to control Luke's life.

Luke had never considered keeping his part of the ranch. He didn't even understand why his grandfather had left him anything. He certainly hadn't been there for Luke when he was a kid, and now that Luke was an adult, he was more than happy to leave that part of his history in the past.

But for the time being, the ranch was a good place for him to take some time to sort his life out. His career in the FBI was still up in the air...and he honestly wasn't sure where he wanted it to land. He'd always taken pride in his work, but he'd become disillusioned with the agency, especially given the way they were trying to make Luke the scapegoat.

Maybe it was time for his tenure at the FBI to come to an end. But that sure didn't mean he'd be coming home to Jessup permanently. That had never been an option.

"I happened to be coming out of the lawyer's office when I heard Kenzie cry out for help. I'm glad I was there."

She nodded, her expression softening as she looked up at him. "Yes, so am I."

"I'm sorry I couldn't catch them, but this isn't the first kidnapping case I've worked. I have some experience in this area. I will find her, Abby. I'll bring her home."

She thanked him, then wiped a single tear from her cheek.

A cloud of failure had hung over him since he'd been put on administrative leave after the death of his team member. He'd been in a fog ever since, unable to function properly or make the right decisions.

No more. He wasn't accepting failure any longer. This was too important.

"Have you noticed anyone hanging around that you don't recognize or who seemed out of place?" he asked as they turned into her neighborhood.

Abby shook her head. "No, I can't think of anyone."

"What about Kenzie? Has she been acting strange or out of character at all?"

Abby sighed and her shoulders sagged. "Honestly, after all she's been through, she's been a trouper. Her behavior has been all over the place until a few months ago, but more recently, I think she's been doing good."

"Caleb will have a team gather security footage from the café and the surrounding businesses. But I'd like to go through Kenzie's room, if that's all right. If she's been talking with someone online, it's possible she's gotten involved in something she wasn't prepared for. She might have known the person who abducted her."

"She's only fourteen," Abby protested.

Luke knew fourteen was plenty old to get involved with predators and fall for their tricks and lures. But saying so wouldn't make Abby feel any better. "It's one angle we need to check out," he told her instead.

She paused, then nodded. "Whatever helps find her. Search anything, look into anything, ask me anything you want to know."

His mind automatically jumped to a handful of questions about their past and why she'd left him the way she did...but he knew perfectly well that now wasn't the time. Maybe later, when her niece was back safe and sound, they could finally talk things out.

If the case *didn't* go well and they *didn't* get Kenzie back safe and sound, then she'd probably never want to lay eyes on him again, much less talk to him. But he couldn't let himself focus on that possibility. Nothing good came from that.

He pulled up to the curb and parked. The front door opened and a young kid of about twelve ran out. That must be Dustin. Abby jumped from the car and met him in the grass, pulling him into her arms. "Aunt Abby, is it true?" he asked. "Johnny down the street said someone hurt Kenzie. Where is she?"

He saw her shoulders slump as she rubbed his hair. "I don't know, honey, but this man is going to help us find him." She turned to

Luke. "This is Agent Harmon. He's with the FBI and he is going to help us bring Kenzie home."

The boy looked up at Luke with tears in his suddenly hopeful brown eyes, but he put on a brave face. "Please help me find my sister."

The kids were the hardest. Luke touched his shoulder. "I'll do everything I can, but I'll need your help. Are you willing to help me?"

Dustin sniffed back tears, then nodded.

"Great. First thing I need you to do is show me to your sister's bedroom."

Dustin motioned for Luke to follow him. Memories of fifteen years ago hit him the moment he passed through the door. The house had been updated since the last time Luke had been there, but remembrances of being here with her still slipped through. Dustin led him to the back bedroom, the one Abby used to have. It didn't look much different now than it had then. Different posters on the wall. Different books on the shelf. But everything still screamed teenage girl. At first glance, nothing stood out to him, but he would have to go through it all with a critical eye.

A laptop sat on the desk in the corner. They would need to have a computer tech dig through it. Teens kept their whole lives online, not realizing the danger it put them in. Whatever trouble Kenzie might have gotten herself into had likely come from her online communications. He'd seen it too many times. Kids didn't understand that predators had gotten good at tricking their prey into believing they were harmless.

He searched through her dresser, finding nothing out of the ordinary. He turned to her bed next and found what he was looking for under her pillow. Her journal. He called Abby into the room and asked her to look through Kenzie's belongings.

"Do you notice anything missing? Any clothes that she might have taken?"

She scanned the room, then shook her head. "I don't think so. Why are you asking me this? It's not like she ran away. Someone took her, Luke. I saw him grab her. So did you. Remember?"

"It's possible she made arrangements to meet up with someone and it turned ugly. It's only a theory, but one we have to consider."

Abby rubbed her face, then shook her head. He could tell this was all pressing down on her. She didn't want to believe that Kenzie could have done something to land herself in this situation. No one wanted to believe that. But more often than not it was true. She turned and walked, returning to the living room. Luke grabbed the laptop and her journal and followed her.

"Don't worry, Abby. Right now, Caleb has his team pulling up tracking information on her cell phone, putting out a BOLO on the car and the man who grabbed her. We will figure this out."

Someone knocked on the front door, causing Abby to jump. He reached for her arms, rubbing them to settle her as Dustin ran to the door.

"It's the cops," he declared as he returned with a uniformed officer.

"I'm Tim Baker. The chief sent me over to set up the trace and go through the girl's computer. You're the FBI agent who'll be helping us?"

Luke shook his hand and introduced himself before handing over the laptop. "It was closed when I came in. Let's go through her emails and online activity. I want to find out who she was talking to and when."

Abby grabbed Dustin's hand and shooed him to his bedroom to start his homework. She walked into the kitchen as Baker set up in the living room. Luke followed her and saw her leaning over the counter. Her shoulders were shaking and her hands were trembling as she attempted to pour a cup of coffee from the pot. He took the pot from her and motioned for her to sit. He poured a mug of coffee for her, then offered Baker one. He refused, so Luke poured one for himself. He needed it, especially after the day he'd had. The impact of the car crash he'd endured was nothing compared to the shock of seeing Abby again after all this time.

He set the mug in front of her, then took the seat opposite at the table. "I'm sorry to do this, but I still need to ask you some more questions. It'll help us decide which way to go in this investigation."

She cradled the cup in her hands, then nodded and looked up at him with sad eyes. "I understand. Go ahead and ask your questions." Her eyes were tired and her expression worn down. But she wasn't going to give up. She'd meant it when she said she would do whatever it took.

"Does Kenzie have a boyfriend?"

Abby gave a small, soft chuckle. "No. She's fourteen."

"A lot of girls her age have boyfriends."

"Maybe, but her parents' deaths put her behind in a lot of ways. She hasn't been interested in boys. At least, she hasn't expressed any interest to me."

"What about her friends? Do you know them?"

"Her best friend is Ashley McDade. They do everything together."

He jotted down the name. "What about teachers or other adults in her life? Has she had issues with anyone, or seemed uncomfortable around them? Maybe you saw something that struck you as odd at the time but now it might make more sense?"

She took a deep breath and tried to think. "I don't think so. Most of my conversations with her teachers were about how she was dealing with her parents' deaths."

Dustin reentered the kitchen. His eyes were red like he'd been crying. "I can't concentrate on my homework. I'm too worried about Kenzie."

Abby pulled him into her arms and brushed the hair from his eyes. Seeing her maternal side was a pleasant surprise. It was a side of her he'd never expected to see. When they were together, she flat-out hadn't wanted to ever be a mother. She'd been too afraid of getting tied down to a small-town life like her mother had. Kids would have only gotten in the way of her ambitions.

That had been a long time ago though. Obviously, things had changed. She might not have had her own kids, but her sister's death had cast her into the role of parent. He thought it was a role that suited her.

Baker called to Luke from the living room. "I finished setting up the tracing equipment, so I started on Kenzie's laptop. You're going to want to see this."

Luke walked over and glanced at the screen over Baker's shoulder. He looked up at Abby. "Was Kenzie adopted?"

Her face paled. "She—she was. Both kids were. Danielle tried for years to get pregnant but couldn't."

"Did she know she was adopted?"

"Yes, she knew. They never hid it from her."

"Baker found a series of messages between Kenzie and a man claiming to be her biological father. It looks like they've been in contact for several weeks now."

"What?" She stumbled backward a bit. He reached out to grab her and she slowly lowered herself to the couch.

"It's possible this is nothing more than a scam, but we need to check this man out."

"He—he's not her father."

"You know that for sure? I didn't even tell you his name yet." He took the spot on the sofa beside her. "Abby, do you know who Kenzie's biological father is?"

She stared into his face. Fear spread across her expression, then sadness. She nodded, then seemed to pull herself together enough to find her voice. "I—I do know."

"The guy she's been chatting with calls himself Adam Lawrence."

She shook her head. "That's not him. He's not her father."

It was obvious she knew more than she was saying and this was not the time to hold anything back. "Abby, I have to know. Who is Kenzie's biological father? What is his name?"

She stared up at him, her chin quivering. "It's you, Luke. You're her father…and I'm her mother." She took in a deep breath. "We are her parents."

TWO

He stiffened at her words, but Abby couldn't quite manage to read his expression. He seemed shocked, certainly, but was he angry? She couldn't tell yet, and she thought that maybe he hadn't made up his mind either. For that matter, she wasn't sure what she was feeling herself. It had been so hard to force the words out. She'd vowed never to tell anyone, especially Kenzie, the truth about her parentage, and she'd made Danielle—the only other person who'd known the truth—promise, too.

She hadn't wanted the burden or the responsibilities of being a mom. It had seemed too overwhelming to even admit the truth.

And now she'd finally said it out loud. Telling Luke the truth was the hardest thing of all to do. Yet she'd known this time had to come soon. Ever since she'd allowed Jesus to turn her life around, she'd known these secrets would have to come out eventually.

Luke stared at her like she'd lost her mind. She reached for his hand when he hadn't spoken in several moments. "She's your daughter, Luke. Our daughter."

Her jerked his hand away, then stood. All the calming reassurance he'd been offering her moments before was gone. She could see anger flashing in his eyes.

He pulled out his cell phone and pressed a button, then pressed it to his ear. "Caleb, find out everything you can on a man named Adam Lawrence. Kenzie has been talking to him online. He's been claiming to be her biological father as a way to lure her in." He gave Abby a cold, hard stare. "Yeah, I'm sure he's not. Let me know everything you find out." He ended the call, then slipped his cell phone back into his pocket and turned to Baker, who was doing his best to pretend he hadn't just witnessed her confession. "Can you take the laptop back to the station and let me know if you find anything else on it?"

Baker loaded up his equipment, then left. All the while, Luke maintained a cold silence and kept his back to her. When Dustin entered the living room, Luke's manner shifted.

He stood beside him and placed a gentle hand on his shoulder. "Hey, Dustin, can you give me and your aunt a few minutes alone? We have some things to talk about."

Dustin looked from him to Abby, then back to Luke. "Is this about Kenzie? Did you find out something?"

His face showed the fear he was feeling, making Abby's heart ache for him. He'd already lost his parents. He couldn't lose his sister now, too. But he was doing his best to be strong and ask the important questions, even if he might not like the answers.

To his credit, Luke's tone was gentle as he answered Dustin. "No. This is about something else. We're still working to find your sister. I'll be sure and let you know when there's any news."

Dustin nodded, then looked at her before he went back to his bedroom and closed the door.

She'd thought she was prepared for Luke's anger, but when he locked eyes with her, she shuddered at the pain behind his eyes. "How could you do this to me, Abby? How could you not tell me I had a daughter all these years?"

She jumped to her feet to explain. "I'm not proud of myself, Luke. I was young and selfish. I know that now. I wanted a life, a career. I didn't want to be tied down to a baby. I was just so scared. I knew you would want us to raise her and that wasn't the direction I wanted my life to go at the time. Danielle and Matt had been trying for a while to get pregnant but couldn't. It seemed the natural thing to do was to give her to them to raise. They were glad to do it and they were good parents. They really were."

He waved away her justification attempt. "You had no right to keep that from me."

She hung her head. "No, I didn't. I'm sorry."

"Did you think I wouldn't understand? Did you think I would be angry? I loved you, Abby."

The anger in his voice had turned to heartbreak with those last words. The intensity of them made tears spring to her eyes, but she blinked them back. "I know. I also know you would have given up everything to be there for me and the baby."

"Of course I would have."

"Don't you see, Luke? That's exactly why I didn't tell you. I didn't want you to have to give up everything you were working for. I didn't want you to have to slink back to this town and work a dead-end job while raising a child. You wanted something more than that for your life and so did I."

Every muscle in his body seemed to clench as he fought to hold on to his emotional composure. "You had no right to make that decision for me."

"I know. I know. It's only been in the last few years since I came here and have had to be a mother to these kids that I realized how selfish I'd been and how completely blind I was to what it meant to be a parent. I robbed myself of that blessing, Luke, but, even worse, I robbed you of even having a choice. I'm sorry."

"You're sorry?" He gave a low, bitter chuckle. "Sorry just doesn't cut it."

She knew it didn't. Even as she'd said the words, she'd known they changed nothing. They were certainly not enough to make up for what she'd done. "I don't know what else I can say. I can't change what I did. I can only tell you how sorry I am."

She wished for something, anything, to make the anger and resentment in his expression go away. But even that was selfish of her. This wasn't about her or making her feel better about what she'd done. This wasn't even about her being able to be forgiven for her actions. It didn't matter if Luke never forgave her. All that mattered now was bringing Kenzie home safely.

She stood and reached for him, her gut clenching when he glared at her hand on his arm. "Please, Luke, you have to find her. You have to make certain she's okay and bring her home." Tears flowed down her face and she didn't try to stop them. "Please, Dustin and I need her. She's all the family we have left. Please. Luke, your daughter needs you."

He pulled his arm from her grasp, then turned and walked to the door. "I'll let you know what we find out." He slammed the door, then got into his car and sped away as Abby watched from the window.

She couldn't blame him for his shock or for being angry with her. She'd been young and foolish and thinking of only herself. Her life was different now. She'd discovered motherhood and found forgiveness in the Lord. Her sister's death had sent her to the lowest depth she thought she could ever go, but God's grace had lifted her back up and shown her the beauty in family and being a parent. She'd been given a second chance, but she'd **completely denied Luke of even his first chance at parenthood.**

All she could do was pray his anger and pain wouldn't be so distracting that they kept him from solving the case. Kenzie had never needed her father more than she did right now.

Abby's words had rocked him.

He had a daughter.

He'd had a daughter he knew nothing about for fourteen years.

And she was in trouble.

His mind whirled with anger and guilt as he drove. He parked in front of the police station, turned off the ignition, but didn't get out right away. Time was not on their side, but he needed a moment to let everything sink in.

He was used to staying impartial on cases. Detachment allowed him to think clearly, logically, and to notice all the details that could make or break a case. He'd witnessed parents getting emotional when their kids had gone missing and, while he'd understood it, he'd wished they'd been able to hold themselves together to provide the information the investigators needed. So many cases could have had a happier ending if the parents hadn't been too locked in grief or fear to share what they knew. Now he was the parent and he didn't even know how he was supposed to respond to this.

Wow.

He was the parent.

A wave of nausea hit him. Not because he'd discovered he was a dad, but because his child was in trouble. Big trouble.

The Meyers case came back to him. It hadn't been the first time he hadn't been able to find a child in time, but that case had shaken him because of the timing. At that point, he'd been thinking about settling down and starting a family.

He and his girlfriend, Tracy, had been getting serious, and for the first time since Abby, he'd started imagining the possibility of building a life with someone else. A life that might actually include children. Abby had never wanted them, but Tracy did, and Luke had started giving the idea some real thought, after a lifetime of being afraid of the type of parent he might become. His examples hadn't been great. He didn't even remember his dad, who'd drowned when Luke was three, but his mother had been neglectful and selfish, so caught up in her own concerns that she hadn't been there for him. The only other adult figure in his life had been his paternal grandfather, who had been more interested in controlling Luke than loving or supporting him. Anything he'd offered had usually come with strings attached and, more often than not, ended up as a shouting match between his mom and his grandfather with Luke stuck in the middle.

He'd sworn he'd never have children unless he was certain he could give them a safe, loving home.

But that fear of not knowing how to provide that had kept him from making that commitment for years, until Tracy. But then the Meyers case had exploded in his face, making the idea of becoming a father seem inconceivable again. Tracy hadn't stuck around long after that, accepting a job across the country and leaving behind nothing more than a note letting him know it was over between them.

He pounded his hand on the steering wheel. Another woman who'd made decisions without consulting him.

He got out and walked inside, finding Caleb in the tech room with Baker, going through Kenzie's computer.

He and Caleb had been close growing up, but they'd drifted once Luke had left town.

"Why didn't you tell me Abby was back in town?" Luke demanded.

His cousin looked rightfully grim. "I didn't

even think of it. I'm sorry. I forgot you two used to be an item."

"I was hoping you were going to say you didn't know."

"I wish I could, but the truth is that I've spoken with her several times. I was the one who called her when her sister and brother-in-law were killed."

After which, she'd come back to take custody of her niece and nephew. Her *daughter* and nephew.

"This guy is definitely not her biological father," Luke told him. "We need to find out everything we can about him. If he made plans to meet up with Kenzie, we need to know about it."

"There's over a hundred exchanges between them," Baker said. "We're still going through them, but it looks like they did make plans to meet."

So he'd managed to lure her to him, then grabbed her? It was a classic ruse that many teens fell for, but why do it on a day when she was out running errands with Abby? And Luke himself had heard Kenzie scream for help. Whatever had happened, things seemed to have gone wrong. But he had her now. The question now was, did he want her for himself or was he part of a group trafficking girls? In that latter case, it was possible this man who'd claimed to be Adam Lawrence wasn't even the same person who'd taken Kenzie. "Let's find out everything we can about this Adam Lawrence, if he's even a real person. Baker, can you track down the ISP he was messaging her from?"

"I'm working on it now."

Caleb motioned Luke into his office. He closed the door behind him and they both took seats. "What's the matter with you? You look like someone just kicked your dog. I know it was a shock seeing Abby again and I appreciate your help on this, but if it's going to affect you this way, maybe you shouldn't be involved."

"No, I have to be involved. I found out something today, something that changes everything."

Caleb folded his arms over his chest, waiting for the news, but the words became stuck in his throat.

"I'm a father. Abby just told me. Kenzie, she's my daughter. Mine and Abby's."

Caleb looked just as stunned as Luke felt. He took a labored breath. "I can't believe she kept that from you."

"I know. I can't even process it right now. All I can think of is finding her. I have to find her."

"Of course. Did Abby tell you anything else?"

"No, but I've seen situations like this before, Caleb. Predators find any way in they can. This guy pretending to be her biological father to lure her in is a classic ruse. He could be a sex offender or even part of a human trafficking group."

Caleb snapped his fingers. "Human trafficking. Abby is working on a story for the local news about human trafficking in small-town America. Apparently, she started researching it back when she lived in Atlanta. She approached me a few months ago asking questions about a ring possibly operating here in Jessup."

"You mean she knew about this and didn't do more to protect Kenzie?"

Caleb flashed him a warning stare. "These people are prepared and most of these teens are reckless no matter how much you warn them about online predators. We've identified several local girls who've been trafficked in the past year. The only problem is that we haven't been able to pin down who is behind it or where they're holding the girls."

"Local criminals or an organized effort?" Organized groups were much more dangerous and tended to move their victims to different states in order to avoid detection.

"We just don't know. We don't have any evidence they're connected to a bigger organization but, so far, they've operated under the radar. We haven't been able to identify them, much less infiltrate them. Abby told me she was continuing her investigation as a side project. She was supposed to get back with me, but I haven't heard anything in months."

He sighed. That meant he had to go back there and talk to her again. At the moment, that was the last thing he wanted to do. He could hardly even stomach the thought of looking at her. But he had to put aside his own feelings and concentrate on the case, on finding Kenzie. They could deal with everything else after she was found.

He stood and straightened. "I'll find out what she knows."

"You don't have to do this, Luke. You can take lead on this from the office. I'll go talk to her."

"No. Not only do I have more experience

in this arena than anyone else on your team, but now that I know my daughter is involved, I can't turn away."

"What are you going to do about her?"

"I don't know. First, I'll need to find her. Then I'll worry about what's going to happen between us."

"I've contacted the local news. I want to do a press conference in time for the morning news programs, get Kenzie's information out there."

"I'll tell Abby to be ready for it."

He headed to his car, or rather, Caleb's car he was still using, and back to Abby's.

He thought about his daughter, how scared she must be now that she realized she'd been tricked. The fact that she didn't even know she had a real father out there looking for her rubbed him wrong. Abby had denied him so much. Kenzie might not even be in this mess if she'd just been honest with him back then.

What would you have done, Luke? Quit college to raise an infant?

He didn't know. But he hadn't had the opportunity to make that choice and that was what angered him most. Abby had robbed him of that.

He parked in front of Abby's house and

got out. The front door opened and she hurried forward, followed by Dustin. They both looked so anxious for answers that he hated that he didn't have any.

He ushered them back into the house. "There isn't any news yet."

"Then what are you doing here?" she asked him. "Why aren't you out looking for her?"

"We're doing our best, Abby. I need to ask you a few more questions."

"Did you find that man Adam Lawrence? Does he know where she is?"

"We're still searching for him. He might not have even been a real person, just a fake profile."

She put her hands over her face and hung her head. "She must be so scared."

Another woman stepped from the living room and introduced herself. "I'm Janet McDade. I live next door."

"Nice to meet you," he told her.

"I've been helping Abby field calls and messages from the press as well as concerned friends from all over town."

"That's very kind of you."

"I'm glad to do it." She turned to Abby. "Why don't I take Dustin next door with me.

He doesn't need to be around all this drama. My kids will keep his mind off of all this."

He doubted that was possible, but one look at Dustin told him the kid was a ball of anxiety. Perhaps a little time just being a kid was what he needed.

Abby nodded and thanked her. "I'll call if there's any news."

She bent and said a few words to Dustin before giving him a hug and kiss then ushering him out the door with Janet.

"There's something I wanted to talk to you about," Luke said once they were gone. He took off his hat and tossed it along with his keys onto the table.

Abby turned to look at him, her face completely void of hope. "What else do you want me to say, Luke? I've already apologized."

"No." He held up his hand. He wasn't ready to have that conversation with her again. Not yet. "This is about finding Kenzie. Caleb told me you were working on a piece about human trafficking in small towns."

She perked up. "Yes, I was. I put it aside after I got the call about Danielle and Matt. After I left the station and moved here, I spent the first year settling in, getting in a good place with my work and good routine with the kids, but about six months ago, I decided to pick it up again. I'm anchoring the news at WKPC, but I was really hoping to pick up some investigative pieces at my old job as a freelancer."

Six months ago was about the time Kenzie had started her quest to find her biological parents, but he didn't mention that. It might be a coincidence—or it might not. "And did you find out anything about any trafficking going on in Jessup?"

Her face fell. "Not much. There have been some people who went missing, but I couldn't prove they'd been trafficked. The story never really went anywhere. Dustin started having trouble at school and Kenzie started acting out. I got so busy that it kind of fell to the wayside."

"So you haven't been investigating?"

"No, not recently."

He rubbed his face and sighed. He'd been hoping she might have a lead or some clue where to start looking for their daughter.

"You don't really believe this has anything to do with me and my story, do you? I dropped that months ago."

He shook his head. He didn't know, but it was one more lead to track down. "Who knew you were pursuing this investigation?"

She shrugged. "Just the general manager at the TV station and your cousin Caleb. Honestly, Luke, the story never went anywhere."

"I believe you. I'd still like to see your notes, if you don't mind."

"I'll email them to you."

He took out one of his FBI business cards he kept with him and handed it to her. "This has my email address on it as well as my cell phone number, in case you need me."

She turned away from him and pressed her hand to her face. Her shoulders trembled and he knew this had her in tears. He placed his hands on her arms and did his best to reassure her.

"I will find her, Abby. I promise you, I will." He shouldn't make such promises. He knew better than most that people went missing all the time and weren't always found. But when it came to Kenzie, he knew he wouldn't give up until he brought her home, where she was safe.

Then they would deal with him being her father.

Abby's sobs racked her body. She spun around and buried her face into his chest. He didn't even think. Just reacted instinctively, wrapping his arms around and holding her as she cried.

He had no idea how long he held her until her tears were spent, but she finally calmed down, bit her lip and stared up at him, her eyes still brimming with tears and her cheeks rosy. Even with evidence of crying, she was just as beautiful as she'd been the last time he'd held her. Possibly even more so. The years had given her a maturity that only intensified her beauty.

As much as he was angry with her, his arms ached for her when she moved away.

She glanced around, eyes catching on the clock on the wall. "I should go next door and retrieve Dustin. It's nearly his bedtime. He'll want me around to comfort him."

It was odd seeing her maternal side, and his heart broke. If she'd been honest about Kenzie, they'd be parents together. She wouldn't have had to go through it alone.

Then he remembered. She'd made the decision to exclude him.

"I should go too," he said, picking up his hat and keys from the table. "I'll call you in the morning and update you on the case."

He turned to leave, but she stopped him, her hand on his arm, her touch sending warm sparks through him. Why did she still have the ability to affect him after all these years?

"Please find her, Luke. I need her to come home."

He held her one last time, even planting a kiss on her forehead before he turned to leave. And he was in his car on the way back to the station before he realized that she hadn't tried to stop him.

Dustin was glad to see her and even happier to come home with her.

"I didn't want to stay at the McDades' house," he told her as they walked back to their place.

"I know you didn't. The truth is that I didn't want to be alone tonight either."

He wrapped his arms around her and she hugged him tightly, soaking in everything about him. At twelve, he was walking that fine line between kid and teen. His hair smelled like watermelon from his Spider-Man shampoo and his skin was soft like only a child's could be. He was still affectionate, giving hugs and kisses at request, while still being a rugged, active boy. Kenzie had always been more aloof with her, especially after her parents' deaths. She'd struggled the most, having to deal with grief, puberty and a new adult telling her what to do.

Abby hadn't been lying when she'd told Dustin she didn't want to be alone. She let him lie on the couch and watch a superhero movie and even joined him with a bowl of popcorn. He fought valiantly through the first hour, but by the end, he was sound asleep. She didn't bother moving him, fearing he might wake up and be unable to go back to sleep. The kid was a knot of nerves and he had every right to be. He'd already lost so much. Both his parents and now his sister too? *God, it's too much.*

She reached for her Bible and tried to work through her Bible study, but nothing made sense to her. Instead, she ended up crying out to God to bring Kenzie back to her, to give her another chance to prove how much she loved her daughter.

When exactly had she started thinking about Kenzie as her daughter and not her niece? She wasn't sure. It was a line she hadn't allowed herself to cross even once she became the kids' guardian. It wasn't until she'd told Luke the truth that she'd finally given up that charade. Only, there was still one person who didn't know the truth yet—Kenzie.

The whole fiasco with Luke was a mess, but it was one she would gladly face head-on if only Kenzie would come home. She would come clean about everything. She'd known Kenzie had been wondering about her biological parents. Her sister had told her Kenzie was asking questions even before Danielle's death. And she'd tried several times to ask Abby about her real mother and father too, but Abby had quickly brushed her off and changed the subject.

She should have known she couldn't keep that conversation on the back burner forever.

Abby dozed on the couch beside Dustin. A noise jerked her awake. She cast an eye around the darkened room. The TV was still playing but Dustin was asleep beside her.

She glanced around. Something was wrong. The hairs on her neck were raised. Something had awoken her, but what? She pushed the blanket away and stood, looking around the living room, then peeking into the kitchen.

She rubbed her hands over her arms as chills ran through her. She tried to calm herself down, to reassure herself that nothing was wrong. Her body was on high alert because of Kenzie's abduction. Her mind was playing tricks on her, making the house feel unsafe even though that wasn't the case.

She switched on the under-the-cabinet light in the kitchen rather than the overhead so the light wouldn't wake Dustin. She turned on the coffeepot and started a cup. She'd only slept a few hours and it was still quite early, but she knew sleep wouldn't come again. She was too worked up, too worried about Kenzie. Her heart ached to hold her and to know that she was unharmed. What must she be going through right at this moment? Was she afraid? Was she crying for her?

She shuddered again. She couldn't go down that road.

A noise from outside grabbed her attention. She hadn't imagined that. She hurried to the window as a figure darted past, the shock of it sending her stumbling backward into the table. She grabbed for her cell phone and dialed the number Luke had given her earlier. He answered on the first ring.

"Someone's at my house," she whispered into the phone.

"I'm on my way. Make sure the doors and windows are locked."

She felt better knowing help was coming, but would he arrive before whoever was outside her window broke in? "Please hurry."

THREE

She rushed to the front door and made certain the locks were engaged. They were. She ran to the back door and did the same. The house was locked up tight. But who would be lurking around her house? And why?

She glanced at Dustin. Surely they weren't coming for him too.

She grabbed a knife from the kitchen. Her hands were shaking with fear but she would defend Dustin to the end if she had to. She took a seat at the kitchen table on high alert.

It seemed like it was forever before she heard a vehicle outside. She hurried to the window and spotted the car Luke had been driving earlier, headlights off, pulling to the curb. He got out and she saw him looking around. She wouldn't feel better until he'd secured the area and determined the prowler was gone.

Minutes later, a knock sounded on her door. "Abs, it's me. Open the door."

She recognized his voice and his nickname for her. She undid the locks and pulled open the door, closing it again and locking it after he was inside. "Did you see anyone?"

"No. Whoever you saw is gone. Hopefully, you frightened him away."

He carefully took the knife from her hand and returned it to the kitchen.

"Do you think this has something to do with Kenzie's abduction?"

"I doubt it. I can't imagine why they would come back here. More than likely it was someone looking for an easy score, unlocked cars or open windows. Do you have any video surveillance?"

"My doorbell has the camera on it. There have been some break-ins in the neighborhood over the past few years, so Matt installed it. I know several of the neighbors have them too."

He nodded. "I'll get Caleb to have an officer contact your neighbors to check their cameras. I'm sure this has nothing to do with Kenzie."

She nodded. Even though she wasn't quite convinced, she knew that he was probably right. She was overly vigilant and everything felt personal and urgent. Her face warmed as she realized how she'd overreacted. She shouldn't have called him. He wasn't in town working to solve burglaries. He wasn't even on official FBI duty. He probably wouldn't want to have anything to do with her if it wasn't for Kenzie.

He took her by the arm and led her to the kitchen table, pulling out her chair and prompting her to sit. "You're shook up. That's understandable."

"You think I made it up?"

"No. I think you're stronger than that, but you've had a long day and a shock." He glanced at his watch. "Caleb wants to set up a news conference for the morning broadcast."

She glanced at her cell phone, noticing several calls from her boss that she'd missed. He'd probably been calling her to set that up. Oh well, she would talk to him at the press conference.

"That only gives us a few hours to prepare. Why don't we go over what you should say."

She nodded, glad to hear he wasn't leaving. She shouldn't have called him but she was glad he was here now. They talked about how she should present herself to the cameras. She was used to being in front of them, but this was different. This was personal and Luke wanted to make certain that shone through. The more she could make the viewers care about her and Kenzie, the more likely they would be to call in a tip if they heard or saw anything suspicious.

As the sun arose, he decided to make breakfast. Abby sipped her coffee and watched as he pulled out a pan, then scrambled eggs and made toast and bacon.

Dustin awoke to the smell of the bacon cooking and entered the kitchen rubbing sleep from his eyes. "What's going on?"

Luke motioned for him to take a seat. "Just a little breakfast before a big day." He set a plate in front of Dustin, then loaded it with scrambled eggs, bacon and toast. Dustin looked at it, then at Abby. He looked like he wanted to dig in, but then she saw what seemed like guilt cross his face. He pushed from the table and took off down the hallway toward Kenzie's room.

Luke glanced at her, confused. "Did I say something wrong?"

She shook her head, then followed after Dustin. He was hugging Kenzie's pillow. "Hey, kiddo. What's the matter? You not hungry?"

"It doesn't seem right to eat while Kenzie is gone."

She put her arm around him and pulled herself close to him. "I know. It doesn't seem right, but it's something we have to do. We have to keep up our strength so we can be there for her when she comes home."

He looked up at her, his soft eyes full with tears. "Do you really think she's coming home, Aunt Abby?"

She pressed her forehead against his and fought back her own tears. "She's coming home, Dustin. I believe it. But you and I have to do some things to help. The police want me to go on TV and spread the word about Kenzie so everyone will be on the lookout for any sign of her."

"You're good at being on TV," he told her. "But you probably need to eat something to keep up your strength." He slid off the bed and took her hand. "We both do if we're going to be strong for Kenzie."

She allowed him to lead her back to the kitchen table. He dug into his food, but despite how good it smelled to her, her stomach was in knots and she only managed to choke down a few bites.

"I talked with Miss Janet," she told Dustin.

"She said you could hitch a ride to class with her and her kids today."

Dustin's shoulders slumped. "Do I have to go? I want to stay here with you."

"I won't be home. I have to go to the TV station for the press conference, remember? Then Luke and I need to go to the school to speak with Kenzie's friends and teachers. Besides, I would feel better knowing you were there. At least I'd know you're safe and being looked after."

Dustin reluctantly agreed to go. "Okay, but will you come to pick me up? I don't want to stay for baseball practice."

"I will. That's a promise." She gave him a high five, then shooed him from the table. "It's time to go get dressed. You don't want to be late."

Dustin grabbed two more pieces of bacon, then ran into his bedroom. She watched him go, her heart aching. "Part of me just wants to keep him here at home so I know he's safe."

"Like you told him, school is probably the safest place for him today," Luke informed her.

"I know. That's why I'm sending him. I also want to keep him in a routine. I think that'll be better for him."

Luke stared at her as he sipped his coffee. "You're good with him."

"He's a good kid. He makes it easy for me, not like—" She caught herself before admitting that she and Kenzie had a strained relationship. It seemed wrong to make that comment now when Kenzie was out there alone and possibly hurt.

Luke set down his coffee mug and reached across the table for her hand. "I remember being a teenager. Fourteen is a hard age. Admitting she's a difficult child doesn't make you a bad parent."

"Imagine being fourteen and dealing with having lost both your parents. She's struggling. That's all."

He should have been railing at her for not taking better care of their daughter. She was definitely kicking herself for it. Luke was giving her much more compassion than she deserved.

Luke looked like he was starting to say something, but his cell phone beeped with an incoming text message before he could. He pulled it out and glanced at it. "Caleb wants us to meet him at the police station. He's made arrangements with your station to set up the press conference there."

She nodded and pushed away from the table. "I guess I should get ready, then." A wave of sorrow swept over her and she pushed her hand to her face. "I don't know how I'm going to get through this."

Luke locked eyes with her. "You won't be alone. I'll be right there with you."

She thanked him, then fled to her room to change her clothes. She wasn't certain if having him there beside her was going to make this easier or more difficult.

Abby was used to facing the cameras heavily made up and plastering on a happy persona no matter what her true feelings were. Today was different. Luke hadn't wanted her to bother with either makeup or smiling for the public. In his words, he wanted the viewing public to see her emotionally distraught over Kenzie's abduction. It would help to personalize her so people could identify with her. He was right, of course, but a part of her was terrified to look so unkempt. She was supposed to be the one who had it all together. Without her protective facade, she felt exposed. She mounted the steps to the podium the TV station had set up and faced the cameras, fisting her hands to try to stop them from shaking.

Chief Harmon greeted the press and established why they were there, recounting the abduction yesterday. "Our department is doing everything in our power to bring this child home, but we need the public's help. Her aunt is well-known in town and would like to address the press."

She stepped to the microphone. She had prepared remarks, but they now seemed hollow and empty. She stared into the camera and imagined she was speaking to one person. It was a trick she'd learned early on in her career. She let the words come naturally, keeping in mind Luke's advice to say Kenzie's name frequently. "This is to the man who took my niece, Kenzie. I'm sure you don't want to hurt her. I've raised Kenzie since her parents were killed in a car wreck two years ago. Kenzie has a little brother who misses her. We both do. We love Kenzie so much and ask that you please just let her go. All we want is our Kenzie back home with us."

She feared she wouldn't get through this as the image of Kenzie's face staring at her from the back of that car hit her.

Luke must have sensed that she couldn't

continue, because he took her arm and led her to take a step back. The police chief stepped back up to add that the Jessup Police Department had established a tip line for any and all information regarding Kenzie's abduction and whereabouts.

Luke took her by the elbow and started to lead her away, but anger suddenly welled up inside her. She couldn't leave it like this.

She pulled away from Luke and stepped back to the podium. She stared into one of the many cameras still broadcasting. "I don't know who you are," she said into the camera, targeting her words at the man who took Kenzie. "You made a mistake when you targeted my niece. You won't get away with this. I will find you." Her tone grew sharper with each word she spoke. "I will hunt you down and I will get my Kenzie back. Do you hear me? I'm coming for you. I'm coming for my child."

Luke grabbed her arm and pulled her away from the microphone and down the podium. "What was that?" he demanded when they were around the corner, out of the press's eye and earshot.

Anger exploded within her. "I just couldn't sit there and beg the man who took Kenzie to bring her home. You and I both know he won't."

"Of course he won't, but that's not why we make those statements. We have to follow procedure."

"I don't care about your procedure. I just want my daughter back!"

His jaw clenched. "You think I don't? I just found out I have a daughter and now I might never get the opportunity to ever meet her. I don't even know the kinds of things she likes or what her favorite color is. I don't know what her laugh sounds like or if she has my personality. All I know is that she's missing. So, I need you to pull yourself together and stay on point so we can find her and bring her home."

Shame and sorrow filled her. He was right. She'd let her emotions get the better of her. She had to remember she wasn't the only one missing Kenzie…or the only one who cared about her.

"Abby?"

She turned to see her producer, George Mason, and her fellow morning anchor, Cindy Davenport, hurrying toward her. They had to have heard the exchange between her and Luke.

Luke took a step forward, obviously intending to send them away. "It's okay," she told him. "These are my coworkers. They're okay." He was trying to protect her, but she was more than a story to these people. They were her friends.

George pulled her to him for a hug and Cindy joined in.

"We were so sorry to hear about Kenzie," George said when they broke their embrace.

"Is there anything we can do for you?" Cindy asked her.

"Just keep putting her name and photo out there on the airwaves."

"Of course we will," George stated. "You're one of our own, Abby. We will do whatever we can to assist the investigation."

Cindy hugged her again. "I'll be praying that she's found safe."

Abby thanked them both. As she watched them walk off, Cindy's comment about praying started to nag at her. Was this God's punishment for how she'd treated Kenzie, abandoning her for all those years? She'd done her best to try to be a good parent since taking on the role. She'd even rediscovered her faith and had been trying to live the way God would have wanted her to. But she couldn't have known God would test her faith so soon after her rededication.

Luke handed her a bottle of water. "Are you okay? Did they upset you?"

She shook her head, then took a sip from the bottle before answering. "No, I'm glad for their friendship. I spent so much of my life going after jobs without considering other people's feelings that it almost feels wrong to have people I consider friends here. Next to God and these kids, they've been my saving grace." He stiffened and shoved his hands into his pockets. "Does it make you uncomfortable when I talk about God?"

He shook his head. "Not at all. I just can't understand it. Your daughter—my daughter—was just kidnapped and her life is in danger. How can you think God is still good after that?"

It was a fair question. "If I didn't believe He was looking over her, I couldn't handle it. I might just fall apart right now."

He rubbed his face. "I wish I could believe as easily as you do. Unfortunately, my experience with the church pretty much mirrored my relationship with my grandfather—tense and commanding."

She remembered how bad his home life

had been. He'd taken the brunt of his mother and grandfather's bickering, with him always stuck in the middle. No wonder he'd grown into such a cynic. She felt her face warm as she realized her rejection had shaped him too.

He sighed and rubbed the back of his neck. "I should go inside to see if any tips have come in from the tip line."

"Already?"

"Someone who watched the broadcast might have called in right away. So far, all the leads we've gotten on the BOLO and the Amber Alert haven't panned out. Caleb and I spent most of last night searching through security video feeds to no avail."

She got his meaning. They needed more information for the case to move forward.

She started to tell him she would do whatever it took to help when her cell phone buzzed. She grabbed her phone and glanced at the caller ID but didn't recognize the number. But she couldn't not answer it, not with Kenzie missing.

"Hello?"

"Aunt Abby?"

She spun around to face Luke. "Kenzie! Where are you? Are you hurt?" She placed the phone on speaker as Luke pulled out his own cell phone.

"I don't know where I am. I'm so scared. Please help me."

"Tell me where you are, honey, and I'll come get you. What do you see?"

"I don't know. They're keeping me locked in a room. I managed to sneak out and find a phone, but I'm scared."

She looked to Luke, feeling helpless to do anything for her. "Try to find a window. Look out and tell me what you see."

"I don't know. I can't—"

Kenzie's scream pierced the air as sounds of a struggle ensued.

"Kenzie!" She reached out for Luke and he wrapped his arm around her. Heavy breathing filled the line. "Who is this? Where are you? Why did you take my niece?"

Instead of answering, the line clicked off.

Abby's heart hammered as Luke grabbed the phone and checked the ID, calling out the number to whoever was on the other end of his phone. "She managed to find a phone and make the call. I want to know who owns that phone and where it's located. This could be our best chance of tracking her down."

He ended the call, then pulled Abby into

his embrace. As he did, she felt his heart pounding as well. "This is good," he assured her. "At least we know she's still alive."

Abby nodded. He was right. She had to focus on that.

Kenzie was alive...at least for now.

Luke planted Abby in the police station's break room while he suited up. He usually kept his gear stored in the back of his vehicle in preparation for FBI raids. Caleb had done him a favor in removing it from his crashed SUV and storing it in one of the lockers. He slipped into his vest and checked his weapons while he waited for data to come back on that trace of the number Kenzie had called from.

He settled onto a bench as he waited. Physically, he was prepared for this, but emotionally, he wasn't certain he was. He'd thought the news that he'd had a daughter had rocked him, but hearing her terrified voice over Abby's cell phone had done him in.

Caleb entered the locker room along with several members of his SWAT detail.

Luke stood and faced him. "Well?"

"We've tracked the coordinates of the call to an abandoned warehouse outside of town."

That was good news. They finally had a

place to search for Kenzie. He picked up his rifle. "I'll go let Abby know. Then I'll meet you outside." He walked to the break room, where Abby was pacing restlessly. "Caleb's team was able to track the coordinates. We're heading there now."

She nodded but anxiousness was flowing off her.

"We're going to find her, Abs. We're going to bring her home."

He checked the urge to embrace her. The real comfort that she needed was the knowledge that her daughter was safe. Nothing else would do until then.

He walked outside and slid into the passenger's seat of Caleb's SUV. He took a fortifying breath. "Let's go."

Caleb drove, leading the team toward the edge of town. He slowed down and cut the sirens as they approached the warehouse. Luke hated to think about his daughter being kept there, but he couldn't focus on his fear for her. He needed to keep his eye on the mission—bringing Kenzie home safely to her family.

They hopped from the SUV and got into team formation. Luke did his best to morph into go mode as Caleb and the others readied to breach the warehouse. He joined in on the second wave, raising his rifle as he rushed into the building.

The place appeared to be empty. No one ran. No one shouted as the building was breached. The criminals could be hiding, but Luke doubted it. The place was too quiet, aside from the footfalls of Caleb's men.

Luke moved to the right and searched through several empty offices before he found a door with several outside locks, none of which were latched. He pushed open the door and spotted a metal staircase that led to a basement area. He descended the stairs, then clicked on the lights. Mattresses were strewn across the room, along with a few blankets and trash items. He also spotted several discarded needles he was certain held drugs used to keep the girls from fighting back against their captors. The room held no windows and the lock on the door indicated this room could be easily secured.

Steps behind him caused Luke to turn and raise his rifle. "Whoa, it's just me," Caleb said, descending the stairs. "What did you find?"

"Looks like somebody was being kept down here. From the looks of it, a lot of somebodies."

Caleb sighed. "We found a pegboard in the

office with photos of multiple girls pinned to it. This place was used by an organization, not a single offender."

Luke agreed with his cousin's assessment. It seemed Kenzie had been targeted by human traffickers. They must have fled when they realized she had alerted someone by calling her aunt.

He spotted something in Caleb's hand. "What's that?"

Caleb held up a small yellow hoodie that looked like something a fourteen-year-old girl would wear. Luke noticed something on the sleeve. He reached out to touch it. Blood.

Caleb gave him a grim look. "I looked back at the notes from my phone from my interview with Abby. According to her, Kenzie was last seen wearing a yellow hoodie."

Luke's heart clenched as he recalled seeing a flash of yellow as Kenzie was pushed into the vehicle by her abductor.

His daughter was in real trouble.

FOUR

As one hour turned to two with no word from Luke, Abby decided she couldn't stay at the police station. No one was answering her questions or giving her any information about the raid. Finally, she asked an officer to drive her home. She could pace the floor in the comfort of her own home as well as she could here.

And, once home, that was just what she did after picking up Dustin early from school. She paced the floor, wringing her hands. What was taking so long and why hadn't she heard anything from Luke and Caleb? She tried calling him but his phone went directly to voice mail.

God, please let Kenzie be okay.

As an investigative reporter, she knew processing a scene took time, but she was going to explode if she didn't hear something soon.

She heard the car pull into the driveway

and met Luke at the front door. The look on his face, plus the fact that Kenzie wasn't with him, sent dread rushing through her. Her heart kicked up a notch as he walked in and closed the door behind him.

"What is it?" she asked him. "What happened?" She was vaguely aware that Dustin had hurried from his room and was now standing at the entrance to the living room, also awaiting the answer to that question. He'd left school early, too worried about his sister to be able to concentrate.

Luke handed her a plastic evidence bag. She turned it over and saw a yellow hoodie with a sunflower painted on it. There were spots of blood on it. "We found this at the warehouse."

She sank to the floor as dread turned to despair. It was Kenzie's hoodie. She recognized it.

"The place was empty by the time we got there. Looks like they cleared out. But this proves she was there."

"There's blood on it." She stared up at him, waiting for him to tell her if there'd been more blood at the scene. "What happened?"

"We don't know that yet, Abby, but we have every reason to believe Kenzie is still alive. We found evidence of other girls and women being kept there too."

That struck her. "You mean like human traffickers?" He gave a slight nod and bile rose in her stomach. What she'd learned in her research on human traffickers had been horrible in the abstract. To think—to know— her child was now in the hands of people like that made her physically ill. Kenzie's life was in danger and their time was limited. "Those rings, they move girls around, some-times sending them across states or even out of the country. She could be gone already, Luke."

"We can't think that way," he told her. "We have no reason to believe she's been moved. That warehouse was some kind of holding facility. They moved everyone, not just her. Moving around several girls puts some big limits on how mobile they can be. We'll find them. Now that we know what we're look-ing for, it'll help to focus our investigation."

She hugged the plastic bag to her as she grappled with this new information. Human traffickers were the lowest of low. People who traded girls and women like property to fulfill their own greed and line their own pockets.

"Abby, I need to take that hoodie to the

crime lab for processing. I only brought this here so you could positively identify it."

She didn't want to part with it. It was all she had left of Kenzie now, but she handed it back to him. As much as she wanted to hang on to it, open it and smell the scent of her, she also wanted every piece of evidence they could get their hands on in order to bring this human trafficking ring to justice.

She stood and stared at Luke, pressing the bag back into his hand. "Promise me you'll find her, Luke. Promise me you'll bring her home." It was unfair of her to lay this burden on him, but she had no one else and he was Kenzie's father. He'd taken on the role of protector without even being asked.

He locked eyes with her and she saw a steely determination in his eyes that she recognized. He could be single focused with something he cared about. He took her hand. "I will find her, Abby. I promise you I will. I'll find her and bring her home. This is what I do."

She had no choice but to believe in him. He was the best and somehow God had brought him back into her life at just the moment she needed him. She had to trust in that.

She watched him go. Dustin came to her,

pressing his frightened young face against her shoulder. He was trying to be strong but Kenzie was all he had left of his family.

"He'll find her," she reassured Dustin and tried to reassure herself as well. "He'll find her and bring her home safely."

Dear God, please let him find her.

Luke dropped off the hoodie at the crime lab. He signed the evidence seal in order to maintain the chain of custody before passing it off to the lab technician.

His whole world might revolve around the results they collected and processed here. He'd been dreading telling Abby about what had happened at the warehouse and it had been worse than he'd ever thought. The look on her face when she'd seen Kenzie's hoodie had nearly killed him.

He took a moment as he climbed back into his car before heading to the police station. He leaned into the steering wheel, doing his best to settle his racing heart. Seeing that warehouse and those filthy mattresses strewn about and knowing his daughter had been there huddled on one of them was like a punch to his gut.

He wasn't even sure how to process all that

had happened to him in the past few days. He'd returned to Jessup to settle an inheritance. Now he'd discovered he had a daughter and that she'd been abducted.

And Abby's casual acceptance of God struck him too. She'd never been religious. In fact, they'd both shunned faith after seeing the hypocrites in their hometown church. His grandfather had been one of the biggest, acting all high and mighty and pretending to be generous while all the while being cruel and petty to his own family.

And that was his only role model for fatherhood. His mother had no siblings, so he'd had no family on her side. He'd had three uncles who'd shown him some kindness, but all of them had passed away while Luke and his cousins were still kids, each one taking with them whatever pieces remained of their grandfather's generosity. Luke didn't know what kind of father he would make, but he'd promised himself that he would never become the kind of man his grandfather was.

He started the car and drove back to the police station. No sense in worrying what kind of father he might be when he may never get the chance to fulfill that role.

He walked into the police station and saw

his cousin huddled with several officers in a conference room. "Have you found anything?" Luke asked.

Caleb stood at the question. "The warehouse has been officially abandoned for six months. The company that owned it went bankrupt, and the bank is looking to sell it. Anyone could have squatted in there. I'm afraid we're not going to get anywhere with that angle."

Luke had been afraid of that. He'd seen how operations like these worked. The men at the head of it were smart, clever, and they took few chances. That was what made them dangerous. And they had his daughter.

"I started gathering a list of all the missing girls and women ages twelve to twenty. If there are others who are part of this ring, then maybe we can follow up on one of their disappearances for clues as to who might be involved."

"That's a good idea," Luke told him. "I'm going to contact one of my colleagues at the FBI and see if they have any leads about rings operating in this part of the state."

Luke had done a lot of work with the FBI's Human Trafficking Task Force during his time at the agency. He knew if anybody had their ear to the ground about trafficking rings, it was his task force team members.

Caleb pulled him aside. "How did she take the news?"

Luke didn't need to ask which *she* Caleb was referring to. "About as well as you would think."

"And how are you taking it?"

Luke glanced at his cousin. He knew Caleb was only asking out of concern, but his question was a dagger through Luke's heart. "I just found out I have a daughter and now she's missing. I'm not fine. I won't be fine until I can bring her home."

"Well, we swept the place for fingerprints and DNA. Hopefully, we'll find something that'll identify the players. We're also canvassing the area and reaching out to other law enforcement agencies in the area for any info on missing girls in their jurisdictions, but information is slow coming in."

"What about the tip line? Any good leads on that?"

"A few came in while we were working the scene at the factory, but they don't look very promising. One is from a local who calls in to the police all the time with complaints. She's always got some new gripe against someone in the community. The other was from a grocery store clerk who claimed to see a man with a girl matching Kenzie's description in his car while he was pumping gas the day she was abducted. I'm going to interview the clerk and pull the store's security feeds. Maybe we can get camera footage of the abductor or at least a good description."

Luke sighed. "We need to start interviewing Kenzie's friends and classmates. She might have told them more about this guy she was in touch with. Maybe something will turn into a lead. I'll take Abby and go talk to her best friend. We'll start there, then branch out." He glanced at his watch. School would be letting out in a few hours. If they didn't get over there before it did, they might have to speak with Kenzie's classmates at each of their homes. Precious time they didn't have to lose.

"I'll head over there now," he told his cousin. "Call me on my cell if there are any developments."

Luke pulled out his cell phone and called Abby to let her know about the plans. It was time to start digging deeper into Kenzie's life, and he knew from experience that he wasn't going to like what they found when they did.

But he would do it if it meant bringing his daughter back home.

* * *

Abby knocked on the door of the McDade residence. Kenzie had been best friends with the McDades' daughter Ashley since third grade and the girls spent a lot of time together. She'd gotten used to seeing Ashley at the house with Kenzie and taking turns with Janet McDade taking the girls back and forth to school.

However, Abby couldn't remember seeing Ashley and Kenzie together for several months now. She'd asked Kenzie about it before her abduction and Kenzie had only shrugged and stated that their friendship was fine. Abby hadn't wanted to press her about it, but she could sense something was going on with her even then.

Why hadn't she pressed her?

Janet's husband, Trent, answered. He gave her a sympathetic smile, then glanced at Luke before opening the door wider. Trent stepped outside onto the porch. "Is this about Kenzie? Ashley was so upset about her that she couldn't even go to school today."

"Dustin told me he hadn't seen her, so I took a chance she stayed home," Abby admitted. "Trent, this is Luke Harmon. He's working with the police department on Kenzie's case. We would like to ask Ashley some questions, if that's all right."

He thought for a moment, then nodded. "Sure. Come on inside. I'll get Ashley."

"She might be more willing to open up if we speak to her in private," Luke suggested. "Perhaps in her bedroom, where she'll be the most comfortable?"

Trent nodded, then led them upstairs. He knocked on a door, then opened it. "Ashley, Kenzie's aunt is here with a friend. They'd like to talk to you about Kenzie." The girl must have nodded, because Trent pushed open the door.

Abby tried to project calm as she walked into Ashley's room. She wanted to do whatever she could to put the shy, sweet girl at ease. Today, she sat on her bed surrounded by frilly pillows and stuffed animals. A book lay open in front of her, but Abby suspected from the redness in her eyes that she hadn't been doing much reading. "Hi, Ashley. It's good to see you."

"You too, Miss Mitchell."

She motioned toward Luke. "This is my friend Luke. He's helping the police look for Kenzie. I guess you heard what happened to her?"

She reached for a stuffed puppy and hugged it. "I heard. She must be really scared."

"She was scared. I heard it in her voice and saw it in her face when that man took her."

"Do you know what happened to her? Is she coming back?"

"We don't know," Luke admitted. "We're trying to figure out why this man would take Kenzie. I was hoping you could give us some insight into what was going on in her life. Was anyone threatening Kenzie or paying too much attention to her recently?"

Ashley pulled on the stuffed dog's ears. "I don't know. Kenzie and I aren't really close anymore—we haven't been for months. Ever since she started looking for her biological father. She became obsessed with it. Then she started hanging around with Tiffany Bell and that group." The pain in the girl's face was evident. "She forgot about me."

That pained statement broke Abby's heart. The two girls had been best friends forever. Abby couldn't believe she would ever forget about her. "Who is Tiffany?"

"She's a junior who started tutoring Kenzie. Juniors don't usually hang around with us, but Tiffany started including Kenzie in stuff outside of tutoring. Before I knew it, she was sitting with her at lunch and spending time with her after school. If anyone would know what was going on with Kenzie, it's her."

Abby thanked her. Then she and Luke left the room.

"I hope she was able to give you something that will help find Kenzie," Trent said as they descended the stairs.

"She was very helpful," Luke said. "She's a strong girl."

"Yes, she is," Abby agreed. "I was sorry to hear she and Kenzie had grown apart. I never thought anything would separate them, but I suppose Kenzie has been going through some stuff since her parents died."

Trent nodded. "I know how hurt my daughter has been, but I understand what Kenzie is going through. I lost my parents at a young age too." He opened the door for them. "Let me know if there's anything I can do to help you, Abby. I hope you find her soon."

"Thank you."

She and Luke walked out and headed back toward her house. Abby was still trying to understand all the changes in Kenzie's life she hadn't seemed to know about. "I knew she was struggling," she admitted to Luke. "I guess I didn't realize how much."

After what she'd put him through, she expected him to accuse her, but he didn't. "Being a teenager is hard. Even in the best of circumstances, people change and grow. Sometimes they outgrow their friends."

"We never did."

She and Luke had been best friends all through school and into college...right up until she'd ruined it.

"No, we didn't. I'm glad for that. I always expected you would discover how amazing you were and wonder why you were spending time with me." He gave her a little smile and a shrug. "I don't know how I would have made it through high school without you, Abs."

She'd felt the same way about him and had considered herself fortunate to be his friend. And when that friendship had blossomed into something more, she'd been happy about that too. She'd imagined so much for their future together, but she'd messed it all up by not being honest with him. When it mattered, she'd only thought of herself.

She saw him stiffen and realized he was probably thinking the same thing. A walk down memory lane would always ultimately lead them right back to her betrayal. A change in topic was necessary. "We need to track down this Tiffany and speak to her. From the sounds of it, if anyone knows about what was going on in Kenzie's life, it will be her."

He nodded. "Let's head over to the school now. Someone there will be able to help us find her." They climbed into the SUV he'd borrowed from the ranch.

East Lake School had been the main school in Jessup for as long as Abby remembered. When she was a child, the county had moved the elementary grades to another school building, but East Lake still contained both middle and high school grades. Both Kenzie and Dustin attended East Lake just as she and Luke had attended all those years earlier.

He parked in the visitor parking space, then leaned back in his seat and took it all in. "This place doesn't look like it's changed at all."

"It hasn't. Not much, anyway."

A flood of memories about their time here threatened to overwhelm her. She did her best to push them away.

She opened her door and got out of the car. Luke followed suit. "We'll have to check in at the front office. Maybe Principal Marsh or someone there can point out Tiffany."

The school's front office secretary was Mrs. Jennings and she'd been at that job since before Abby and Luke attended East Lake. She also knew Abby from her frequent visits to handle the kids' matters—and possibly from TV—and greeted her by name.

"Hello, Abby. I hope Dustin is feeling better."

Mrs. Jennings was the one who'd called earlier to say that Dustin had wanted to be picked up early and taken home. "I'm afraid it's just all too much for him," Abby explained.

"The poor boy has been through a lot with losing his parents. Now this mess with Kenzie." The secretary shook her head and gave her most remorseful expression. She glanced at Luke with a quizzical look. "What can I do for the two of you today?"

"Mrs. Jennings, do you remember Luke Harmon? He went to school here the same time I did."

Her eyes widened and a smile brightened her face. "I certainly remember you, Luke. You're all grown up now, aren't you?"

"It's nice to see you again, Mrs. Jennings."

"I was sorry to hear about your grandfather's passing. I assume that's why you're back in town?"

"Yes, ma'am."

Abby noticed his jaw clench at questions

concerning his grandfather. That had always been a touchy subject for him. "We're here, Mrs. Jennings, because we're looking for a girl that Kenzie had been spending a lot of her time with. Her name is Tiffany Bell, and I believe she's a junior."

"Oh, of course. Tiffany tutors a lot of the younger girls. She's very sweet. What do you want with her?"

"We're speaking with anyone who knew Kenzie well, hoping to get an understanding of who she was interacting with and who was in her life prior to her being abducted."

"Of course. I did notice she and Kenzie had been spending time together." She typed something into the computer and then nodded. "It looks like Tiffany is in the chemistry lab for last period." She glanced at the clock on the wall. "However, the last bell is about to ring. You might do better searching for her as she leaves. She usually parks in the front parking lot."

"The problem is that I don't know what she looks like."

Mrs. Jennings smiled and pulled out a yearbook from a stack on the desk. She flipped through it, then slid it across the desk to them and pointed out a photo. "That's her. That's Tiffany."

Tiffany Bell was a pretty girl with dark hair and a big smile. Abby thought they shouldn't have a difficult time finding her.

The bell rang and the halls suddenly filled with noise and bodies all heading toward the exit.

"Thank you for your help, Mrs. Jennings."

Luke held the door for Abby and they pushed into the hallway. His height was helpful among the crowd of students. Abby did her best to scour through the crush of kids to try to spot Tiffany, but there were so many.

"There she is," Luke said, pointing.

She followed his lead and saw the very person they were looking for.

Abby hurried across the lot and onto the sidewalk as she caught up with Tiffany. Luke followed behind her. "Tiffany!"

The girl stopped and turned at the sound of her name. She plastered on a cheerful smile. "Yes? Can I help you?"

"My name is Abby Mitchell. I'm Kenzie's aunt."

Tiffany nodded and her smile faded. "I heard what happened. It's terrible. Poor Kenzie."

"I was hoping I could ask you a few questions. Her friend Ashley told me you'd been spending a lot of time with Kenzie lately?"

"That's right. I've been tutoring her in English literature. The school's counselor asked me to do it. She said she was getting behind in her academics since losing her parents. I was glad to help."

Abby wasn't aware Kenzie's grades had been suffering. They'd never been great since Abby had taken guardianship of the kids, but she'd chalked it up to grief. And it wasn't like Kenzie had been failing her classes—at least, not that Abby was aware.

"Did she say anything to you that stands out? Someone she was speaking with that she shouldn't have been?"

"No, I'm sorry, she didn't. She spoke a lot about missing her parents, but other than that, we worked on Shakespeare." She gave them a sorrowful smile and a shrug that seemed less than genuine.

The girl was lying. Abby felt it in her bones. Ashley had told them Kenzie was spending a lot of time with Tiffany. They couldn't have been studying the entire time. Tiffany was hiding something.

Abby tried again. "It's my understanding that you and Kenzie spent hours together.

Lunch together. After school. You two must have talked about *something* besides English lit."

The girl shifted her books and looked uncomfortable. "I've already told you most of our conversations were about schoolwork. I liked her but we weren't friends."

"I've heard differently," Abby pressed. "I've been told that you two were inseparable even after school. It seems odd that someone in your grade would associate so often with a freshman, especially with your friends."

"Look, I like Kenzie and I felt sorry for her."

"So you did spend time together."

Luke pulled out his FBI credentials and showed them to her. "We're investigating a possible connection to human trafficking. We could really use your help to find out what was going on in Kenzie's life. Was there a boyfriend? Someone paying too close attention to her?"

Tiffany pushed a strand of hair behind her ear. She looked put on the spot and Abby was certain she knew more than what she had said so far.

"You do understand that if you lie to an FBI agent, you could go to jail," Abby warned her. They had to keep pressure on her.

"Tiffany!" A woman about Abby's age walked toward them. She stepped between Abby and Tiffany. "I'm Shyla Porter, the school's counselor. What's going on here?"

"I'm Abby Mitchell and this is Luke Harmon. My niece is Kenzie Hall. As you must have heard, she was kidnapped and I was told she'd been spending a lot of time with Tiffany. We were just asking her some questions."

Ms. Porter turned to Tiffany. "Why don't you head home."

The girl nodded, glanced at them, then turned and walked swiftly toward the parking lot.

"You shouldn't be questioning her without her parents present," Ms. Porter insisted.

"We weren't interrogating her," Luke insisted. "We only wanted to uncover any information she could share about Kenzie."

"Mrs. Jennings in the office knows we're here."

Ms. Porter seemed unaffected. "I asked Tiffany to tutor Kenzie. As far as I know, that was the only reason the two of them spent time together."

"With all due respect, Ms. Porter, we've heard differently."

Ms. Porter folded her arms and shot them a

surprisingly irritated stare. "Look, I'm sorry about what happened to Kenzie. I pray she's found soon, but you can't come on campus and harass other people's kids. I can't allow that. Besides, Tiffany is a good girl and an excellent student. She puts herself out there to help other students. Attacking her isn't going to help you find Kenzie."

"Do you know Kenzie?" Luke asked.

"I do. I speak with her often." She glanced at Abby. "It's no secret that she hasn't been adjusting well since her parents' deaths. She was falling behind. I tried to help her."

"Why wasn't I contacted about this? If she was struggling, I should have been notified. I'm her guardian and this is the first I've heard about it."

"I did what I thought was best for her. She didn't feel like she could talk to you or about how unhappy she was at home. I was trying to respect that. Now, if you'll excuse me, I really have to go."

As she walked away, Abby turned to see Tiffany driving off. Ms. Porter had managed to keep them occupied until she'd gone.

"What do you think?" Luke asked her.

"I think Tiffany was lying to us and I want to know why."

He nodded. "I have to agree. She's hiding something. It might have to do with Kenzie."

"We should keep an eye on her."

Luke agreed. "But not on school property. Ms. Porter is correct. It's one thing to ask other kids about Kenzie, but, if I suspect them of something, I can't legally question a minor without a parent present."

"Maybe you can't, but I can. No one is going to come after me for trying to find information on my missing niece. And I'm not stopping until I get answers. Tiffany is involved in this. I'm certain of it. I'm going to keep my eye on her. Maybe she'll lead me to whoever it is that has Kenzie."

Tiffany Bell had gotten away from her this time, but Abby was determined to uncover what it was she was hiding. That girl might be the key she needed to find Kenzie and bring her home.

FIVE

Luke dropped Abby back at her house, then returned to the police station. She was distraught over not getting the answers they'd been looking for, but there wasn't much more they could do at the school today.

He decided to turn his attention to Caleb's investigation into the theory that the other missing girls in the county were tied to the trafficking ring.

He approached his cousin as he entered the building. "How did your interviews go?"

"Nowhere. How about you and the interviews with Kenzie's friends?"

"We spoke to her former best friend, who claims she's been spending a lot of time with an older girl, Tiffany Bell. We tried to talk to Tiffany, but she seemed evasive. The school counselor shooed us away before we could get any real answers."

"Tiffany Bell." Caleb jotted down the name. "I'll do a background check. Maybe she's had a run-in with the law that could give us some leverage to get answers out of her."

He hoped so too, but he wasn't holding his breath for that. Like Abby, he did believe she knew more than she was telling, but, if she was involved, she was probably more frightened of the people in charge than she was of law enforcement. She'd hardly reacted to hearing the FBI was involved. He chalked it up to her just being a kid and having no understanding of the weight an FBI investigation commanded.

Although, he wasn't even working in an official capacity and he wasn't so sure he ever would again. He was technically on leave at the moment, and his time with the agency might very well be coming to an end.

He wasn't so sure he wanted to return even if they allowed him to after the official inquiry.

Caleb approached Luke with a sheet of paper in his hand. "These are the names of all other missing girls in the area spanning the whole county, including three different schools."

Luke glanced at the names on the list.

Twelve sets of parents missing their twelve daughters. He understood how they felt now in a way he never had before. But one aspect of this situation bugged him. "Why did they kidnap Kenzie out in public, in broad daylight like that? Most girls are lured into these rings. They come willingly to some meetup location, and from there, they are drugged or threatened into the back of a car or a van to be spirited away without anyone seeing them. They're not taken off the streets and stuffed into the back of a car in broad daylight." That was the part that didn't make any sense to Luke. He'd never seen anything like this before. What was it about Kenzie that had made this group so bold?

He stared at the list again and at the different schools these girls attended all in the same county. He imagined there were several more lists like this throughout the rest of the surrounding area. This ring was active and working. The oldest disappearance was over eighteen months ago. Less than one disappearance a month, and all the rest of the girls reported missing when they didn't come home. With the exception of Kenzie, that was exactly what he would expect from a trafficking ring. They were lying low. Luring their victims in.

They may have intended to do that with Kenzie as well, perhaps with Tiffany at East Lake School as the bait to reach out to the targets, to get to know them and groom them for the criminals. Tiffany certainly seemed to have invested a lot of time into Kenzie. So what had gone wrong? Why had she been grabbed?

He borrowed a computer from Caleb and video conferenced with Amy Pearson, a colleague at the FBI.

Amy smiled when she came on the screen and saw him. "Luke, good to see you. How are you doing?"

"Hi, Amy. Good to see you."

"I heard you were taking some time off. After Nashville, I can't say I blame you. I heard what happened. We're all sorry for your loss."

Luke rubbed the back of his head. He hadn't called to be reminded about his most recent mess-up. It was a memory he was trying to push away. "Thanks, Amy. I actually called because I'm back in my hometown of Jessup, Texas, and there've been several girls gone missing. We have reason to believe it's human trafficking. I wanted to find out if your department had gotten any intel on such a ring in this area."

He heard her tapping on the keyboard. "It looks like we have had some calls come into the national hotline from that area. Several missing girls. We farmed out the tips to local law enforcement, but it looks like most were classified as runaways." She gave a loud sigh. "One or two runaways is understandable, but this many in one cluster area in such a short period of time raises my radar."

It raised his too. "I'm looking at a list of twelve girls gone missing in this county alone. They're spread across three different schools, in different parts of the county. All in the past eighteen months."

"I'd say that's the best indication that you've got something going on there. Are the locals calling us in?"

"Not officially. I know the guardian of one girl that was taken off the street, so I offered my help to the local police."

"Off the street? That's unusual."

"I know."

"And the police are open to your help?"

"They are. My cousin Caleb is the chief of police here in Jessup."

"So you're assisting him?"

More like he was assisting Luke. Officially Caleb was the law in this town. But Luke had taken over the moment he knew his daughter was involved and Caleb had been happy to let him take the lead. He knew Caleb was a capable chief of police and had a good team of officers under his rank. But none of that mattered when his daughter's life was at stake, and they both knew that Luke was the one with the experience to get her back safely.

"Well, we've seen some spikes in missing girls. I'll forward you all the data I have. Let me know if you need anything else."

"Thanks, Amy. I appreciate it." He ended the call and waited. The email Amy promised came through minutes later. He spent the next few hours searching through it, memorizing it all.

She was right about there being a definite spike in activity in this area in the last eighteen months, but that wasn't new information. He read through the list of rings known to be operating in Texas but couldn't find anything that pointed to a specific one as being more or less likely to have snatched Kenzie off the street. If they hadn't traced Kenzie to that warehouse, he wouldn't even be investigating this angle. He would be treating this case as a straight predator abduction.

But they *had* traced that call from Kenzie to the warehouse and *had* seen evidence of a trafficking ring.

Luke turned back to the list Caleb had given him. He picked out a name from the list of missing girls and scrolled through the file on the computer, noting several things that struck him as odd. Most teenagers these days had cell phones and this girl was no different. However, her cell phone activity had changed after she went missing. It hadn't stopped completely, but it had slowed down a good bit. Checking the other files, he noticed the same trend in their cell phone records. The kidnappers had probably taken the phones from the girls to use them for their own purposes before dumping them.

In four of the cases where the girls had been classified as runaways, the parents had actually received a text message from their daughters letting them know they had decided to leave town. The messages appeared to come from each girl's phone; however, all the parents believed someone else had written them.

Luke pulled up several of the text messages. The wording in all were very similar. Too similar to be a coincidence. He made sure an alert was set up on each of their phones to let them know if they were ever turned back on again. He had to admit, though, that he wasn't very hopeful.

He was doing everything he knew to do to bring his daughter home, but it didn't seem enough. It was frustrating. He'd never been so personally affected by a case before. This was one he couldn't let go cold. He couldn't give up. He was looking for a girl whom he didn't even know, yet he loved her. He loved the very idea of her. And the memory of hearing her cry for help nearly crippled him, nearly sent him back to that dark place he'd been after Nashville, when his teammate Michelle had been murdered. He'd killed the bad guy but it had been too late. His hesitancy had cost Michelle her life. He couldn't allow that to happen with Kenzie.

Her heart-shaped face stared back at him from her photograph taped to the wall. He'd placed it there to help him remember, to re-mind himself of what he was working for. Yet he couldn't help noticing the little familiar details of her face. Abby's nose and mouth. His baby blue eyes. He didn't need a DNA test to know that Abby had been telling the truth. This girl was his daughter.

He swallowed hard, thinking about Abby and her betrayal. He'd loved her so much. To know she'd concealed something so important from him hurt, and he didn't know if he could ever forgive. He tried not to dwell on it; however, each time he stared at the picture of Kenzie, he felt Abby's betrayal like a punch in his gut.

He wasn't sure what he was going to do when this was all over and Kenzie was home safely. He couldn't consider that now. All he needed to focus on was doing all he could to find her.

But his eyes were drooping and the words on the screen were beginning to mush together. He needed sleep and food. He'd looked through all the evidence Amy had sent over and set up a work area to process it. He'd soaked in all the information until his eyes gave under the strain. He needed to regroup. Come back fresh. It was only late afternoon, but he hadn't slept in days and it was catching up to him.

He turned off the computer, stood and grabbed his jacket. "I'm heading to the ranch," he told his cousin. "I'll be back in a little while."

Caleb nodded and promised to let him know if anything happened while he was gone. He walked out to his borrowed SUV and climbed inside. He headed out of town toward Harmon Ranch. Memories began to flow back to him with each place he passed.

Mostly bad memories, but there were some good ones too. Abby Mitchell featured prominently in a lot of the latter.

It should count for something. Only it didn't. He wasn't sure anything was going to be able to make up for the way she'd let him down.

Abby couldn't get the thought of Tiffany from her mind. She was sure Tiffany knew something about Kenzie, and Abby couldn't let it go without knowing the truth.

She paced the house for a while, frantically cleaning to try to push thoughts of Kenzie away, but it didn't work. She couldn't just sit around and do nothing while her daughter was in danger and there was a lead to be tracked down. Maybe Luke had to follow the letter of the law when it came to leaving Tiffany alone, but that didn't mean she did.

She'd seen Tiffany's car as she drove away, but that didn't do her any good. It wasn't like she could drive around town searching for a dark-colored two-door coupe. But she might be able to narrow down where Tiffany and her car might be.

She opened up her laptop and clicked on a social media site. She searched for Tiffany's name and found her page easily. Abby noted she was friends with many of the same people Kenzie was friends with, which wasn't surprising. She scrolled through the multiple posts detailing many aspects of Tiffany's life—school, friends, hangouts. She jotted down several of the hangout places before she found what she was looking for. A post about working part-time for Buck's Auto Repair Shop. She even listed the days and times she worked.

Abby glanced at her watch and realized Tiffany would be at work there now. She grabbed her keys and hollered at Dustin that she was going out for a while and would be back soon, before hopping into her car and driving to Buck's Auto Repair Shop.

She took in a sharp breath when she spotted Tiffany's car in the parking lot. She was here. And if Abby followed her long enough, she might lead her to where Kenzie was being held.

She parked on the street and surveyed the place. It was an older building on a corner lot. Cars in all states of disrepair were housed behind a tall chain-link fence, and two garage bays faced the street, while large windows showcased a lobby area. Abby spotted several men coming and going from the garage bays, but she didn't see any sign of Tiffany through the windows.

After about an hour, when Tiffany's shift was scheduled to end, the front doors opened and Tiffany walked to her car.

Her purse was on her shoulder and she was looking at her phone as she walked. However, before she reached her vehicle, she glanced up and spotted Abby.

Abby did her best to duck but the damage had been done. Tiffany had seen her. She stopped, then turned and hurried back into the building.

Abby tensed and gripped the steering wheel. Tiffany knew she'd been watching for her. She thought she'd been discreet but obviously not.

Oh well. No use hiding it anymore.

She reached for her purse, readying to get out to go confront Tiffany again. The girl obviously didn't want to talk to her, which made

Abby more determined than ever to find out what she knew.

She opened her car door then closed it without getting out as a man walked out of the garage and crossed the street. He was walking with determination and headed her way. Abby tensed and wondered what to do. Her initial instinct was to drive away. It would be the safer choice. But she'd come for answers, and she couldn't stomach leaving without them, even if it put her in danger. She spotted Tiffany standing at the window with her arms folded and her face grim.

The man was big and bulky with wide shoulders and a menacing walk. He stopped at her car and knocked on the window.

She let it down a smidgen.

"What are you doing following my girl, Tiffany?" Even his tone was demanding and unfriendly.

She took in a steadying breath and did her best to keep her hands from shaking. She couldn't let a little intimidation run her off. "I'm looking for my niece. She's gone missing." She reached into her purse for a photo of Kenzie and held it up to him. "I believe Tiffany knows more than she's telling me about what happened to her."

He nodded at the photo. "I know her. She's been around a few times with Tiff."

Abby's heart clenched at the thought of Kenzie hanging around this place and this man. He was at least in his midtwenties and looked to be a rough sort. But at least it was confirmation of what Ashley had said, that Kenzie and Tiffany had been spending lots of time together, and not just at school.

"You know Kenzie?"

"Lady, it's none of your business who I know. Just like you have no business hanging around here."

"Someone abducted her. Pulled her off the street."

"It wasn't me and it wasn't Tiffany. She told me how you and a fed accosted her at school. You'll leave her alone if you know what's good for you."

Abby gulped at the implied threat. This was a turning point. "I won't until I know what happened to my niece. I won't ever stop looking for her, Mr. . . . .?"

"Lewis. Pete Lewis. I own this place and it's an honest shop. I won't have you hanging around here harassing my customers or my employees."

"Who have I harassed?"

"Tiffany."

"She works for you?"

"Now, what did I say about *my* business being none of *your* business?" She couldn't help but feel uneasy at the look of threat on his face when he leaned in.

"You know, I'll bet your niece wasn't kidnapped. She probably ran away from you. She probably couldn't wait to get away."

Abby's gut clenched at his words. They hit too close to home. With all the conflict between them lately, it was possible Kenzie had said some terrible things about living with Abby. But Kenzie hadn't run away. That abduction hadn't been staged. She'd seen the terror in Kenzie's face and heard her cries for help—on the street and then in her phone call. Her little girl hadn't left on her own and Abby wouldn't stop until she found her.

Her phone rang in the holder on the dash and Dustin's face showed up on the screen. She glanced at the clock. Time had gotten away from her.

It was time to go.

Lewis grinned. "You'd better hurry home and take care of that kid before you lose him too."

His laugh sounded cruel and mocking as

Abby started the engine and pressed the button to roll the window back up. As she drove off, she noticed Lewis watching her through her rearview mirror. She had a bad feeling about him. Worse than the one she'd gotten from Tiffany. Had they done something to Kenzie together? He wasn't the man who'd grabbed Kenzie off the street, but that didn't mean he wasn't involved.

She gripped the steering wheel tighter and choked back tears at the entire situation. Her baby was in trouble and she was confronting people she would much prefer to stay far away from. People who Kenzie apparently knew and spent time with—all while Abby had no idea. How had her life gotten so turned around?

Dustin phoned again and she answered the call, letting him know she was on her way home. She couldn't allow him to worry. He still needed her. But she meant what she'd told Lewis. She wasn't giving up on Kenzie either. Wherever her child was, she was going to find her and bring her home.

Dustin looked tired the next morning as they prepared to leave for school. She thought he might want to stay home again, and she probably would have been okay with that if he'd tried to convince her to let him, but this time, he was determined to go.

Still, the slump of his shoulders as he climbed into the car bothered her.

"Are you sure you're up for this? It wouldn't hurt anything to stay home today."

He shook his head, then tossed his backpack into the back seat. "I'll be fine. Turns out, staying home means I have more time to think about Kenzie."

She started the car and backed out of the driveway. Things were tense between them because of Kenzie, but Abby was picking up some different mood in Dustin. He looked especially down today.

"Is everything all right? Do you want to talk about what's going on with the investigation?"

He shook his head, but she didn't miss the slight tremble of his chin.

She reached out and touched his arm. "Dustin, what is it? What's wrong?"

"It's not a big deal," he said, but she didn't believe a word of it.

"Then it shouldn't be a big deal to tell me what it is. Come on, honey. I can take one look at you and see it's not nothing. Please tell me what's going on."

"Everyone's talking about what happened with Kenzie."

Abby stiffened. She wasn't sure she wanted to know what kids were saying about Kenzie's abduction, but she needed to hear it if it offered anything useful. "What are they saying?"

"It was all over social media last night. People kept sending me messages. They say she ran away from home to meet her biological father. That she didn't want to stay here anymore. They're claiming she staged the whole abduction thing." His chin quivered again and she saw him fight back tears.

She reached over to him. Kids could be so cruel, and in the land of social media, truth didn't seem to matter much. "You and I both know that Kenzie loves you. She would never choose to leave you behind, Dustin. You're her family."

"I knew she was looking for her real father. I didn't understand why she wanted to find him. Why Mom and Dad weren't good enough for her. Why I wasn't good enough for her."

"Honey, being curious isn't a crime. Kenzie was grieving, missing your folks and hoping to get something back. But that has nothing to do with you or the way she felt about you."

Tears wet his lashes and he quickly swiped his hand over his eyes. "I just miss her," he said, his young shoulders and head hanging low.

Abby wanted to pull him into her arms and comfort him, but stopping in the middle of early morning traffic wasn't exactly the place for that. Besides, he would surely push her away if she tried. She could get away with cuddling him when they were at home, but not here where people—particularly his classmates—were watching.

She headed for the school to drop him off, and then she intended to swing by the television station. Her boss had been understanding about her taking some time off, but being away from the office would just make things pile up on her desk. It would be good to take some time to look at paperwork while she waited for Luke to phone her with an update on the case. Besides which, she wanted to use the station's resources to do a deeper dive on Tiffany Bell and her boss, Pete Lewis.

Dustin pushed earbuds into his ears and tuned her out as he fought to control his emotions. It was quiet in the car. A quiet that was, unfortunately, familiar. There had been a time when Kenzie would have been chatting about her life and her friends and which boy liked which girl, but for the past six months, Kenzie hadn't been as chatty in the mornings. Abby, to her shame, had actually enjoyed having a more peaceful drive where she could collect her thoughts before starting the day. But now the silence was horrible, and she'd give anything to have Kenzie's chatter back.

Abby pushed away that train of thought. She couldn't focus on what she didn't have or what she'd missed. She had to put all her energy and all her focus into taking care of Dustin and finding Kenzie. Nothing else mattered but these two kids.

Learning that Kenzie had more than likely been abducted into a human trafficking ring had rocked her. She knew how dangerous those organizations were and exactly how much trouble Kenzie was in. They had to find her and quickly.

She thought about talking to her producer about going on the air with the information she'd compiled on human trafficking rings—but her research was nowhere near ready to be compiled into a story yet. If she claimed that she was absolutely certain Kenzie had been abducted as part of a human trafficking ring, she could get the network in trouble for broadcasting speculation as fact. They simply needed more information about this trafficking ring before they plastered the news of it all over the county.

However, it was possible that a personal appeal might work. She could plead with the other parents around the area whose children had gone missing—or who were in the process of being groomed, as Kenzie had been. They might know something that would lead back to Kenzie's case. If they could pool their resources together, they might stand a chance of finding and saving their kids.

She was focusing on this new idea when she noticed a car came up behind her. She didn't think anything about it. Kids sped through this part of town often. Especially this time of day, with traffic headed to the school. But this one didn't slow down. At least, not until it reached her. Then it rode her bumper.

She tapped her brakes, slowing down. He could go around her if he was in that much of a hurry. He was probably trying to beat the train that came through this intersection at about this time every morning.

But to her surprise, he continued to ride her bumper instead of passing her.

She pressed the brakes again to stop as the train whistled in the distance and the arms began to lower.

The car behind her hit her bumper, pushing Abby's car forward toward the tracks.

She pressed the brakes as hard as possible but couldn't stop. Another vehicle roared up beside her, blocking her path, while another stopped on the other side of the tracks. The car behind her rammed her hard, metal crunching as the more powerful vehicle forced her car to break past the barrier arm and slide up onto the tracks. From there, there was no way to pull forward, given the pickup on the other side.

Panic gripped her. The car wouldn't move and the whistle of the train grew closer.

Dustin braced beside her, his face grim with fear as he stared over at her. "Aunt Abby, what are we going to do?"

She glanced through the side window at the train approaching.

No time to panic or work out a plan. "Jump!" she told him. "Get out of the car."

He grabbed the handle and pushed, but nothing happened.

"It won't open!"

She tried her door and found the same

thing. The impact of the car behind them seemed to have knocked everything in the car out of alignment—including the doors. Even the windows wouldn't respond when she tried the button to roll them down. They were trapped inside.

Their only hope was to either break the windows or crawl out the sunroof.

She pushed open the sunroof—murmuring a prayer of thanks when it opened. "Go, go, go," she yelled. He darted through the small opening, then turned back to her. "Get off the tracks," she told him. "Don't wait for me."

Once he was clear, she pushed her upper body through the opening and was greeted with the vision of the train heading her way and the sound of the whistle blowing and the squeal of the train's brakes. She was sure the conductor was trying to stop, but at the speed the train was going, it wouldn't be able to halt before it reached her car.

She saw Dustin waiting alongside the tracks as several men hopped from the vehicles that had blocked hers on the tracks and climbed into the car that had rammed her from behind. It took off.

"Aunt Abby, hurry!" Dustin called.

She pulled herself up and climbed onto the

roof of the car as the train barreled forward. She slid down the back, hitting her head on the bumper as she tumbled to the ground, just barely clear as the train rammed into her car, pushing it down the line and sending bits of metal flying.

Abby covered her face and rolled into a ball to protect herself as best she could. Smoke and metal rolled over her. Sharp bits stung at her arms and back as the massive train roared to a stop.

"Aunt Abby!" Dustin ran to her. She pulled him to her and hugged him, then made sure he was okay.

"Are you hurt?" She checked his arms and legs, but he'd gotten through this ordeal un-scathed.

"You're bleeding," he said, his voice choked.

She spotted drops of blood on her arms and legs, but it was nothing life-threatening.

She hugged Dustin to her again, a mix of relief and terror pounding through her veins. This had been no traffic accident. Those cars had boxed her in and pushed them onto the tracks. This had been an attack on their lives and by the grace of God they had survived it.

Suddenly, the world started spinning. Dustin looked over at her, but his face was blurring and everything was getting dark. Her head hurt and all she wanted to do was close her eyes.

The panic on Dustin's face was enough to tell her that something was wrong with her. His eyes widened and his mouth came open. "Aunt Abby? Aunt Abby, what's wrong? Are you okay?"

All she could think about at that moment was how he'd already lost two parents in a car wreck. That fear shone brightly on his face and she wanted to reassure him that everything was going to be fine, but she couldn't get the words out. She couldn't even move.

"Aunt Abby? Aunt Abby, are you okay?"

The darkness pulled her under before she could even respond.

SIX

Luke was pouring himself a second cup of coffee and trying to wake up when Caleb burst through the kitchen, pulling on his boots and jacket. The clench of his jaw and utter despair on his face told Luke something terrible had happened.

"What is it?" Luke asked him.

"Train versus car on Route 17."

He knew that crossing. It was a dangerous one, with regular trains coming through and very few safety measures. "Anyone hurt?"

Caleb slipped on his hat. "I don't know. I just got the call from Dispatch but, Luke, you should get dressed. The caller who reported it was Abby's nephew and they called an ambulance to the scene."

Panic shot through him so strongly that he felt frozen in place for a moment. He quickly pushed past it, dumped his coffee into the sink—he no longer needed it—then ran to his room to grab his boots, hat and coat. He slipped them on in the car as Caleb drove to the scene.

His breathing stopped altogether for a moment when they rounded the curve and he spotted the train jackknifed and what remained of a car crushed against the front of it. Caleb parked as close as he could get to the ambulance. Luke hopped out before he even had the truck in Park, hurrying toward the ambulance. The scene was chaotic, with fire personnel dealing with the train and its crew. Metal scraps were strewn at least a hundred feet or more, and the look of Abby's car—he was sure it was hers crunched in front of the train—nearly gave him a panic attack. No one inside at the moment of impact could have survived that.

He scanned the scene until he located Dustin huddled on the grass, a blanket around him. Luke ran to him. "Dustin, are you okay? What happened?"

The boy was shaking from the trauma and shock but managed to tell him, "These trucks blocked us in and pushed the car onto the tracks. We had to climb out through the sunroof. Aunt Abby almost didn't make it out before the train hit us. Then she passed out right in my arms."

"Where is she now?"

"The paramedics loaded her into the ambulance."

"Stay here. I'll be right back. I'm going to check on her."

He darted toward the ambulance and only drew a breath again when he spotted Abby lying on a gurney inside. "How is she?" he asked the paramedic tending her.

"She's got some minor injuries and I think she must have hit her head when she climbed out of the car. We're transporting her to the hospital."

"Luke." The weak way in which she said his name rocked him. She'd nearly died today and his heart was still racing from hearing the news and seeing the devastation she'd survived.

He stepped into the ambulance and took her hand. "Abby, you're going to be okay."

A tear slid down her cheek. "This is my fault. I did this."

"No, you didn't."

"They're trying to keep me from looking for Kenzie. I told them I wouldn't give up."

Her meaning hit him and he stiffened.

"What do you mean you told them? Who did you tell? And when?"

"Last night. I found out where Tiffany worked and I went there to confront her. A man came out instead and warned me off. I told him I wouldn't stop looking for Kenzie and he threatened me."

Anger burned through him. "Who did, Abby? Give me a name."

"He said his name was Pete Lewis."

"Was it him? Was he the one who pushed you onto the tracks?"

"I don't know. I didn't really see them. I only saw the train. But I know he had something to do with this. It must have been some kind of warning or a way to shut me up."

Luke was heartened to see that fire back in her eyes. It made him feel better that she still wasn't easily intimidated. And he had every intention of checking out this Pete Lewis. "Okay, let's not jump to any conclusions. We'll figure everything out. For now, let's get you and Dustin checked out by the paramedics."

He couldn't stop the pang of concern he felt for her as he climbed out of the ambulance, but he chalked it up to him needing her to find Kenzie. It had nothing to do with his lingering feelings for her...because he didn't have any. Anything he'd felt for her had been shattered by the discovery of her betrayal.

Sure it did. That was why he'd been a nervous wreck on the way here.

But how could he ever care for her after what she had done, what she had hidden from him?

Now that he knew she was going to be okay, his anger toward her rekindled—not because of the deception this time but because of her recklessness. Abby had placed herself in a dangerous situation by following Tiffany and nearly gotten both herself and Dustin killed.

He pulled the paramedic aside. "What about Dustin? The boy?"

"No injuries that I can see, but we still need to take him to the hospital to be safe."

Luke hurried over and got him. "Your aunt's going to be fine, but you both need to be looked over by a doctor. I'll meet you there."

He nodded and climbed into the ambulance. Luke saw him take Abby's hand before the doors closed.

He took a moment to catch his breath as the ambulance roared away. Then he turned back to the scene and found his cousin.

"Dustin said these trucks surrounded them and pushed them onto the tracks." The vehicles were still there, abandoned by their drivers.

Caleb rubbed his face, then nodded. He'd probably been hoping against hope that this had been a simple malfunction or something like that—just bad timing, with nothing malicious or targeted behind it. At least, that was what Luke had been hoping for.

"None of them have license plates and one of the responding officers is certain there was a report early this morning about a stolen vehicle matching that pickup."

"This was a coordinated effort," Luke said, realizing it himself the moment the words left his mouth. "They planned this."

"They probably watched her. Knew she went this way every morning. This train comes through here every morning at the same time."

Luke felt ill at the depravity of people.

"Did Dustin recognize any of the people?" Caleb asked.

"I don't know. He was in shock. I'll ask him more at the hospital."

Caleb nodded. "You go ahead. I'll clean up here." Caleb tossed him his keys. "Take my car. Again."

He was going to owe his cousin a lot once they got through this.

Luke arrived at the hospital emergency room and found Dustin in the waiting area, his arm in a sling. "Are you okay?"

He stood and nodded. "I jarred my shoulder, but nothing's broken. The doctor said I just need to ice it and it should feel better in a few days."

"What about your aunt?"

"I haven't heard. The nurse told me to wait here and someone would come get me when I could see her."

Luke saw fear in Dustin's face and remembered that his adoptive parents had died not too long ago in a car accident. While Luke didn't know the details of that event, he was sure that the circumstances had to make this situation doubly scary for Dustin. He put his hand on the boy's shoulder. "Abby is going to be all right. You saw her for yourself—she was fine. Just a little banged up. Okay?"

Dustin nodded. "I know. I keep trying to tell myself that, but after everything that's happened—"

"You don't have to explain," Luke told him. "I'm going to go see what I can find out. I'll be right back."

He walked down the hallway toward a nurse's desk. He pulled out his FBI credentials and showed them to the nurse on duty. "I'm checking on Abby Mitchell. She came in after a train hit her car."

The nurse pointed him toward a room down the hall. He hurried to it, pushed it open and found Abby lying on the hospital bed. She was hooked up to an IV and her arm was wrapped in a bandage. For a moment, his heart skipped, and a swell of emotion rose up in him. He pushed it away when she turned to look at him.

Her smile was weak but warm. "Luke. You're here."

"How are you feeling?"

She sat up on the bed. "I'm okay. Just sore. How's Dustin?"

"He's fine. I just left him in the waiting room. He's worried about you."

"I want to see him. The nurse was supposed to go get him, but I think she got busy."

Luke went and got Dustin and brought him into the room. He ran to Abby and hugged her, his concern apparent.

"I was so worried," Dustin said.

"I'm okay. We're both okay."

"What did the doctor say?" Luke asked her.

"They believe I hit my head on the ground when I rolled off the car and that's why I lost consciousness. They want to keep me overnight for observation, but I told the doctor I couldn't do that. I have to be there for Dustin."

"You have to take care of yourself," Dustin told her. "I can stay next door with the McDades. I'll be fine."

"I agree with Dustin. You need to rest so that you can recover," Luke told her. "I'll make sure Dustin is taken care of."

She hugged Dustin again, then nodded. "Okay, but call me when you get there and call me again tomorrow to let me know you made it to school."

"I will. You take care of yourself, Aunt Abby. I can't lose you too."

She touched his face and Luke was struck by how obvious it was that she cared a lot for this child. She wasn't faking her concern for these kids. She truly loved them and wanted to do what was right for them. She'd given up everything she'd fought for in order to return home to care for them. That had been a big sacrifice for her.

Luke turned to her. "I'll let Caleb know you're okay. He'll want to send someone over here to take your statement about what happened."

She nodded. "I'll be here."

"I don't guess I need to tell you that your car is totaled. I'll come by tomorrow to take you home."

"Thank you, Luke. And thank you for looking after Dustin for me."

He nodded and stuffed down his desire to hug her. He couldn't allow his emotions to get the better of him. In order to stoke his frustration with her, he decided that now was as good a time as any to address her recklessness.

"This could have turned out much worse, you know. Not to mention what could have happened to you last night if Lewis had decided to attack you instead of just making you uncomfortable. I need you to make me a promise that you won't go off on your own again. That you won't put yourself in harm's way. That you'll let me and Caleb and the police handle this from now on."

She didn't respond right away and he saw conflict on her face. "I promise to consult you next time, but I can't promise not to be involved. This is my daughter." Tears filled her eyes. "I'll do whatever I have to do to bring her home."

He could tell that this was the best he was going to get. This attack hadn't deterred her. She would do whatever it took to find Kenzie, even if it put her in harm's way. He didn't know whether to feel proud for her spunk or angry at her recklessness.

He arranged for a hospital security guard to watch her room, then drove Dustin to their house to pack a bag. Luke watched him as he walked next door and briefly spoke with Mrs. McDade to let her know what had happened to Abby.

"I'll take care of him," the neighbor assured him.

"Thank you. Abby should be back home by tomorrow."

He gave Dustin his cell phone number and told him he would check on him later, then drove to the police station to touch base with Caleb.

His cousin had collected video surveillance from the intersections around the train tracks. "I'm hoping to get more information from the vehicles that were involved. All of them have been confirmed stolen last night. I'm hoping we can identify who was driving them."

"Have you found anything yet?"

"The videos just came through. I haven't had a chance to watch them yet."

"I'll take care of it," Luke told him.

He spent the next few hours looking through footage. Some, like the video surveillance from the bank in town, provided better-quality images, but together they were able to blanket the intersections leading to the train tracks and show where the vehicles involved went through.

He spotted Abby's car. Then identified the others pulling in behind her.

Luke keyed up the image. He couldn't make out the drivers of any of the vehicles well enough for a description, but these images confirmed that these men had targeted Abby. They had followed her, boxed her in and then forced her onto the train tracks. They'd planned this.

It could have some connection to Abby's visit to confront Tiffany and the man who'd warned her off, and he would definitely follow up on that lead, but this could also just be connected to the trafficking ring and their need to get her out of the way to stop her search for Kenzie.

He sighed and stared at the image of the driver of one of the vehicles.

Who are you?

Discovering the identity of these drivers might be the key to finding out who was targeting Abby and where he could find his daughter.

Abby felt the pain of her ordeal the next morning. She was stiff and her muscles sore. In the moment, she'd been too caught up in shock and adrenaline to feel any pain, but that had all faded now, leaving her with plenty of aches—along with plenty of worries.

She didn't take what had happened lightly. Someone had tried to shut her up for good. Someone had tried to make sure she didn't continue her search for her daughter. But she didn't intend to relent in her search, no matter how much danger it put her in.

She did her best to hide her pain from the nurses as they prepped her for discharge, but she couldn't wait to be home to down some Tylenol and soak in a hot bath to work out the kinks in her muscles.

She was dressed and ready to go when Luke arrived. He looked handsome but tired, and she knew it wasn't fair to place this burden on him. She'd made this mess, but she needed him to find Kenzie, so she was glad he was here. She'd also been very impressed with how gentle and patient he'd been with Dustin. She'd never had a reason to question his parenting skills, only her own.

"Thank you for driving me home."

He nodded. "I talked to Dustin on the phone this morning. He seems to be holding up. He said he was going to school today."

"Yes, I spoke with him too. He wants to give me time to rest and recuperate, but I think he really just wants to get back to a normal routine."

"That makes sense. Kids need routine."

It was odd not seeing her car in the driveway when Luke parked in front of her house. That was another thing she was going to have to figure out—how was she going to get around until she could replace her car? The thought of dealing with insurance companies and car salesmen made her head hurt even more so than her concussion.

As he had been several times before, Luke was already on top of it. "I called the rental company and they'll deliver a rental car here for you to use this afternoon. Although, you probably shouldn't be driving with a concussion."

She waved away his concern. "It was a

minor injury. I'm fine. Thank you for taking care of that."

"Well, it was obvious your car wasn't going to be able to be fixed. There wasn't much left of it. You and Dustin were very fortunate not to have been seriously injured or killed."

No one knew that better than her. "We weren't fortunate, Luke. God was watching over us."

He flashed her a skeptical look, then shook his head. She expected him to make some sort of comeback, since she knew he was struggling with the whole faith aspect, but he obviously decided it wasn't worth the fight.

"What's happening with the investigation?" she asked to shift the conversation. "Did you find out who did this?"

He shook his head. "All of the vehicles involved were stolen and the video cameras that picked them up weren't clear enough to get an identification on any of the drivers. Are you sure you can't identify them or give a description?"

She thought back but nothing came. They were just blurs of people working to cause her harm. She'd been too focused on searching desperately for a way out to pay much attention to them. "I was so focused on the train that I didn't really see their faces. Did you talk to Lewis? I'm sure he was behind this."

"Not yet, but I can't just accuse him of attempted murder without proof. So far, there's nothing to tie him to Kenzie's abduction or to pushing your car onto the tracks. I'm heading over there to question him, though, this afternoon."

"I want to come," Abby insisted.

He shook his head. "No, you're not coming with me. Your accusations will only make his defenses go up. I know how to handle an interview. Let me do my job."

She backed off. "Call me after you talk to him," she called to Luke as he left.

He assured her he would, then got into his SUV and drove away.

Abby closed the door and locked it. She pulled in a deep breath. Luke was right. She needed to let him handle this. He was, after all, the professional and had more experience with criminals and abduction cases than she did.

Only, letting go was so hard when her daughter's life was at stake.

Luke keyed the address for Buck's Auto Repair Shop into his GPS and followed the directions. It led him to a part of town he was familiar with. The lot with the auto repair shop used to house a general store back when he was a kid. He remembered shopping there with his mother because the prices had been low and the owner sometimes offered credit to his regular clients…for an incredibly high interest rate.

Luke gripped the steering wheel at the memory. It still angered him that his mother had scrimped and saved to raise him while his grandfather lived in wealth only a few miles away and never lifted his hand to help them—at least, not without strings attached.

He parked and got out, walking into the garage area. Several heads poked out from beneath the hood of a car. He pulled out his FBI credentials and held them up for everyone to see. "I'm Agent Harmon with the FBI. I'm looking for Pete Lewis."

A man came out of the office wiping his hands on a rag. "I'm Pete Lewis."

He was short and stocky, and his shaggy beard and tattoos gave him a rough appearance. "You own this place?"

"I do. What does the FBI want with me?"

"You had a confrontation with a woman the night before last, Abby Mitchell."

"The lady in the car. I remember. She was harassing one of my employees. Why do you ask?"

"Because she was nearly killed yesterday. Her car was pushed into the path of an oncoming train. Do you know anything about that?"

He shrugged. "That's the first I've heard of that. I didn't have anything to do with it."

"Where were you yesterday morning at seven a.m.?"

"Sleeping. I partied late the night before. Woke up at eight and opened the shop at nine."

"Can anyone verify that?"

"Verify that I was asleep at seven?" He shook his head. "I was alone. But I'm telling you, I had nothing to do with what happened. All I did was warn her to leave Tiffany alone. I was just trying to be a good boyfriend."

"Tiffany Bell is your girlfriend? I thought she just worked for you."

"She does, but we've been going out too."

"Isn't she in high school?"

The guy shifted his feet. "So what? She's seventeen and I'm only twenty. I inherited this place from my father when he died two years ago. You want my whole life story or is that enough?"

Luke didn't care for the attitude, but he

didn't have any more questions. At least, not any that he thought the man would be willing to answer.

As far as the business itself went, it didn't appear to be just a front for illegal activity. There was every indicator that it was a functioning garage based on the cars in the bay and the people working on them. He'd run a background check on Lewis, which showed a few run-ins with the law, but they were mostly petty thefts, robberies and bar fights. He certainly didn't strike Luke as sophisticated enough to operate a human trafficking ring. On the other hand, however, he could see this guy rallying his friends to attack Abby and Dustin on the road. He'd come across his type before. The kind of man who would blitz attack you in a dark alley instead of a face-to-face brawl.

But how did he and Tiffany connect to a trafficking ring?

It was a question he was asking himself as he left the shop, climbed back into his car and drove away.

Abby wasn't happy when Luke's call came and he didn't have the news she wanted to hear. He'd questioned Lewis and looked into his background and didn't see anything to indicate that he was connected to the trafficking ring that had snatched Kenzie.

Despite his findings, she was still convinced Tiffany was the key to finding her daughter.

She picked up Dustin from school, and then they spent the evening watching a movie together. Until a few days ago, he would have normally been too busy with his video games and chatting with his best friend to pay her much attention. She knew he was only spending time with her now because he was worried and because he needed reassurance that she was still there and wouldn't be leaving him too. She was okay offering him the additional attention he needed. She didn't want to get so caught up in finding Kenzie that she forgot about his needs too.

But after he departed to his bedroom, she turned her attention back to the investigation. Luke had filled her in on the details. No camera footage of Kenzie's abduction, no viable footage of the men who'd attacked her and Dustin, no leads on the trafficking group. She sighed. They were at a standstill.

She went to bed feeling defeated. Her body ached from her injuries, but her mind and heart were devastated. She did her best to remain positive and optimistic, but each day that passed without a word about Kenzie made her wonder if she would ever see her again.

She finally drifted off to sleep after tossing and turning for hours.

Something woke her. Abby raised her head from the pillow and glanced around. She thought she'd seen a shadow in her room. She glanced around but saw nothing. It had probably been part of her dream, her unconscious playing into her fears and anxieties. Still, she doubted she'd be able to get back to sleep. She glanced at the clock. Even if she had only managed to sleep for three hours.

She pushed back the covers and stood. She was awake now and going back to sleep wouldn't be an option. She walked down the hall to Kenzie's bedroom door and touched the nameplate and pretty flowery cutouts she'd decorated it with. The aesthetic was a throwback to happier times in her life, times when Danielle had been alive. She'd been such a nurturer, a natural mother to her kids. Abby had a lot of regrets about giving up her child, but none about letting her sister care for Kenzie.

She opened Dustin's door and peeked inside. He was asleep on the bed, his headphones in and music blaring. He wouldn't hear an earthquake if it happened.

At least he was safe.

She couldn't say the same for Kenzie.

She walked into the spare bedroom she was using as an office. She didn't bother switching on the top light, as the streetlamp outside the window provided adequate illumination. Besides, she wasn't sure she was ready to face the harshness of the overhead yet.

She clicked on her laptop and opened her social media sites. She'd joined a local group for missing teens, a place where family and friends could exchange information and sightings and details. She'd added Kenzie's information to the site earlier today before she picked up Dustin from school. She clicked on the post she'd made and read through all the comments. There were a lot of regrets and prayers that Kenzie would be found quickly, but no pertinent information.

The sound of glass breaking grabbed her attention. She jumped to her feet and hurried into the hallway. The odor of smoke and gasoline was strong. She walked into her bedroom and saw flames blazing on the carpet, her bed and the curtains, and the window was broken.

Her house was on fire.

She ran to Dustin's room and pushed him awake. He groggily blinked his eyes open. "What's going on?"

"There's a fire. Let's get out of here." They needed to exit the house then call the fire department before the fire spread out of control.

He hopped from the bed and Abby hurried back into the hallway toward the front door.

Another loud crack pierced the air and fire blazed nearly in front of her. She gasped, grabbed Dustin and turned him back toward his room. A quick glance at the front window showed a large hole and a dark figure running away.

Someone had tossed a firebomb through her front window. Probably that was what she'd heard earlier too from her bedroom.

They had to leave the house now, but their exit was blocked.

"We're going to have to get out another way," she said.

She pushed him back into his bedroom and closed the door. Smoke was already heavy and she knew they had to escape soon. She went to his window and pushed on it, trying to open it, but it wouldn't budge beyond a certain point. She pounded on it as frustration and fear pulsed through her. It was an old house and she couldn't remember the last time anyone had even tried to open a window.

"Dustin, see if you can squeeze out of here."

The opening was small but Dustin was young and thin. If anyone could get out, it would be him. He slid through, having to push once to clear the opening. Abby knew there would be no way she could get through it.

"Run next door and call 9-1-1. Get help."

"Your turn, Aunt Abby," he said.

"I'm not going to make it that way," she told him. "Go. I'll find another way out."

She tried pushing open the window again but it wouldn't move. The frame must have warped—or maybe the window was designed to only open partway.

She saw the fear in Dustin's eyes and told him again to run and get help. He finally, reluctantly, did.

Well, if she couldn't get out through the window's opening, she would have to break the pane. She grabbed Dustin's desk chair and rammed it into the window. It didn't break, so she hit it again and again until it cracked.

Smoke billowed in from under the door. Abby knew she needed to get low and cover her mouth, but she couldn't do that and break this windowpane. She needed to keep working at it—but she also needed something easier to lift. Her strength was waning. She dropped the chair and picked up something smaller, the bedside lamp, and began pounding at the crack on the window until it splintered and broke. She tossed the lamp aside and climbed out, her arms and legs catching on the jagged edges.

She fell to the ground, then scrambled away from the house, coughing and staggering. She didn't feel safe until she felt the cool of the grass beneath her.

Dustin came running to her. "The fire department is on the way. Are you okay?"

She wanted to reassure him she would be fine, but she couldn't stop coughing long enough to speak.

Moments later, the roar of the fire truck sirens sounded. She staggered around to the front of the house and collapsed on the driveaway. A duo of firefighters came to check on her and Dustin as the others turned their attention to the house.

"Is anyone else inside?" one of the firefighters asked her.

She shook her head no. She glanced at the

house that had been in her family for years. She'd grown up here and now it was being destroyed.

She walked with the firefighter to an ambulance when it arrived and allowed them to give her and Dustin a checkup. They administered oxygen and bandaged the cuts she'd sustained from crawling through the window.

Moments later, a vehicle screeched to a halt, and she spotted Luke leaping out from behind the wheel. He glanced at the house on fire, then scanned the area. When his gaze landed on her at the ambulance, his face paled and he blanched.

He walked over to them. "Are you both okay? I heard the call on the police scanner and recognized the address."

"We're okay," she said, hugging Dustin close to her.

"How did this happen?"

She saw the question in his expression. He was hoping this had started as a simple grease fire that had gotten out of hand or possibly even bad wiring. She hated to disappoint him. "Someone threw something into the window of my bedroom, then again through the front windows. It smelled like gasoline, and I think it was already on fire. The flames spread fast and nearly blocked us inside."

His jaw clenched at that news. "A Molotov cocktail?"

She nodded. "I think so. I heard something break and went to investigate. That's when I saw the fire."

He looked back at the house. Flames were enveloping most of it. All her memories were inside. Memories of her childhood, her parents, her sister, even Dustin and Kenzie's memories...ones that would be even more precious if they couldn't find her.

"Someone did this deliberately," she said. And she had a good idea who. Pete Lewis. He'd threatened her and even tried to have her run over by a train. Now the fire. Well, this wasn't going to stop her.

"What are we going to do now?" Dustin asked, sounding so much like a little boy that she wanted to pull him into her arms and comfort him.

"We'll figure something out," she said, choosing to rub his back instead.

Luke leaned in. "You two can come stay at the ranch."

"We couldn't put you out," she started to say, but he was quick to reassure her.

"It's no bother. You know that place has plenty of room. Besides, I'd feel better knowing you were in a safe place." He stared back at the house and she caught his meaning.

This was no accident. This was an attack against her that was intended to be lethal. They were no longer safe at their home. Her attackers had just tried to kill her for the second time. No doubt they would try again.

"Thank you. We accept." She shot Luke a thank-you smile. The ranch was large and Luke was right about there being plenty of space. Dustin would enjoy the horses too and the sprawling land. Plus, he would be safe there. She wouldn't have to worry about him. No one would get on the ranch without being seen by the ranch hands and security feeds.

As she watched her house burn, she realized these people had just upped the danger level. The more she tried to find Kenzie, the more they would come after her. She had no choice but to focus on keeping Dustin safe now.

SEVEN

The paramedics insisted both she and Dustin go to the hospital. She agreed to go but didn't care for the many hours they had to wait to be treated. They needed to get to someplace safe, and she didn't think the hospital security would be enough to protect them. At the very least, she didn't think they'd have any peace of mind while they were there. The worry on Dustin's face was real and troubling. He'd seen her trapped inside that house and had feared losing her. She needed to get him someplace where he could truly feel safe.

She couldn't help thinking of Kenzie. Where was she tonight? How safe did she feel? How long would it take before they were able to bring her home? But then she found herself wondering what kind of home Kenzie would be returning to. No house. All of their possessions gone. And would Abby and Kenzie still be at odds with one another?

She was glad to see the smile on Dustin's face when they climbed into Luke's SUV after leaving the hospital. At least one of her kids was still happy to be with her—even if she could see some tension and anxiety hovering behind his smile. She was thankful Luke was here but she could see too he was worried about her. For that matter, she was worried about him. She doubted he was all that happy to be back on the ranch—a place that held so many unpleasant memories.

As children, they'd spent a lot of their time running and climbing around the grounds, the barns and outbuildings when they were there, anything to stay away from the main house and the people inside. As he got older, Luke often even refused to step foot there. His resentment for his grandfather and how the old man had treated him and his mother was a deep and real wound.

She watched his body tense as they drove beneath the sign that announced they had entered Harmon Ranch. It was a sprawling five thousand acres with livestock.

The house was massive too. It contained twelve bedrooms and spoke to the wealth the

Harmon name engendered. It had been built by Luke's great-grandfather and added on to through the years. She knew that it had once been filled with family back when Luke's father and his siblings had been alive. However, losing all four sons had taken a toll on Luke's grandfather Chet Harmon. It had turned him into a cold and bitter man who clung too hard to what little family he had left. Unfortunately, his cast-iron determination to claim what was his didn't work as well with people as it did with livestock. From what she knew, he'd managed to push away all the family he had left except for Caleb, the one grandchild who'd stuck by him. Abby wasn't sure why.

She remembered Luke's grandfather as an angry, resentful sort of man. Generous to the community at large but not to his family. She'd witnessed the fights and arguments between him and Luke's mom. He'd wanted to control Luke's life but his mother had prevented it. She wouldn't allow Luke to be under Chet's thumb, not after the way he'd abandoned them following Luke's father's death, and not unless she received something in return.

Luke parked in front of the house and they got out. They had saved nothing from the house except for themselves, so they'd stopped by a store after leaving the hospital to grab some necessities, a change of clothes and new cell phones to replace the ones they'd lost in the fire. Luke paid for it all and his generosity warmed her.

He led them into the house and up the stairs. He opened a door and flipped on a light.

"You can have this room all to yourself," he told Dustin.

He walked to another room and opened that door. "This one is for you. I figured you would want to be close to Dustin."

"Yes, I would. Thank you."

"My room is at the end of the hallway. Caleb is on the other side of the house, so you should have some privacy."

"Thank you for letting us stay here, Luke." She set down her bags and turned to him.

"You're welcome. I'm glad you're here. I feel better knowing you're both staying here." He closed the door to give them privacy from Dustin in the next room down. "I spoke to the fire chief. There's no doubt this was arson."

She rubbed the gooseflesh that rose on her arms. "I knew that. Someone intentionally set fire to my house."

"We'll figure out who did this."

She sighed and sat on the bed. "I think we both know who did this."

He nodded. "I know you believe Pete Lewis is involved."

She nodded. "I believe he's responsible, even if he didn't throw the Molotov cocktails himself. But how do we prove it?"

"I've got the police canvassing the neighborhood to see if anyone saw anything. Caleb is also going to try to locate any video surveillance that might identify our arsonist. The real problem might be trying to tie it to Lewis. If he is involved, I doubt he's the type to get his hands dirty himself for something like this, but I suspect he knows plenty of people he can hire."

She rubbed her arms again. "What does that say about how Kenzie is being treated?"

"You can't obsess over that, Abby. We have to hold on to the hope that she's okay until we can find her. Human trafficking rings are notoriously organized, and nothing about Lewis screams 'organized' to me. My best guess is that, if he is involved, he hires the muscle for someone else."

"I pray you're right." He stiffened at her

words and grew uncomfortable. "What's the matter?"

He shook his head. "Nothing. I know it's just an expression."

"What?"

"Praying. You don't—you don't really pray to God, do you, Abby?"

"Absolutely, I do. I need Him now more than ever." She didn't know how she would get through this without God and His strength. She was barely hanging on even with it. However, she could see Luke was struggling to even understand. He had a right to his anger and resentment toward her, but she hadn't thought about what learning about Kenzie, then about her abduction, would do to his faith. It had never been strong. Even when she'd known him all those years ago, he'd held on tightly to his anger, which had gotten in the way of accepting the idea of Grace. She'd hoped that would have changed in the years, but it was obvious now that it hadn't. She'd had the privilege of finding forgiveness through Jesus Christ. He, obviously, hadn't.

It was understandable that he might wonder how she could cling to God after all this.

"I'll let you get some rest. Feel free to use the kitchen if you want. Hannah is the housekeeper. She keeps the kitchen fully stocked. I'm not sure who she thinks she's stocking it for anymore, but she does."

"Thank you. I'll need a way to get Dustin back and forth to school. I'm sure my new rental probably isn't drivable any longer."

"No, I'm sure it's not. You think he needs to go after last night? He won't have any of his stuff."

They'd spent hours in the emergency room making certain both her and Dustin's lungs hadn't been affected by the smoke inhalation. After stopping to buy things they'd needed, the day had gotten away from them and Dustin had already missed most of the school day. "I'll feel him out to see what he wants to do, but I think school has become his safe place. You're right though. I'll have to replace his backpack, notebooks, computer and sports equipment."

He nodded. "I'll make arrangements for the rental company to drop off another car." He shot her a grin. "Good thing I got the full insurance package, huh? Who knew we would need it so soon?"

She knew he was attempting to lighten the mood, but her face warmed. If the rental place knew what had happened to her car, they probably had insisted on the full insurance package for her rental.

He walked out and closed the door behind him. She unpacked the few belongings she'd purchased, then sat on the bed as tears threatened to explode from her. She let them come. If Lewis had wanted to destroy her, he'd come awfully close.

But he hadn't succeeded in killing her. He'd only managed to strike a chord in her that made her more determined than ever to find out where Kenzie was and to bring her home.

Luke went to his bedroom and fell into a chair. He sighed and rubbed his eyes. They still stung from the smoke of the fire, but it was his emotions that had been taking a beating the last few days. He wanted so badly to hold on to his anger toward Abby, yet each time she found herself in danger, all he did was worry about her.

And it was more than simply nostalgia or a concern for the safety of the mother of his child. Panic had gripped him again at the idea that something might have happened to her. That he might never see her smile again or hear her voice.

A part of him that he'd thought was long

buried—the part that longed to start a family—had sprung back to life, and here was one almost ready-made for him to step into. But how could he ever get past her betrayal or her stubborn reliance on faith in a God who allowed so many terrible things to happen?

His daughter hidden from him, then abducted.

Abby and Dustin nearly killed by an oncoming train, then a fire.

Michelle Simmons's murder by a vicious killer without Luke being able to stop it.

He did his best to push Michelle's death from his mind, but it refused to budge, everything about the memory reminding him that it was his fault. She shouldn't have died. He'd been there, raiding the abductor's home. They'd had him cornered physically and with enough evidence to put him away for life. They should have been able to prevent him from taking any more lives...but they hadn't.

He hadn't.

Jack Shelton had abducted and murdered six women before they'd uncovered his identity, but his final victim had been a twenty-six-year-old federal agent he'd grabbed from behind and used as a human shield. Luke had hesitated at taking the shot, wanting to take him in alive but also afraid of hurting Michelle, and Shelton had seen his chance to claim one more victim, slitting her throat before Luke could fire his weapon and end his reign of terror.

He stood and pulled his hands through his hair. Everything that had happened to Kenzie, to Abby, to Michelle.

Where was God in all of that?

Nowhere.

If He existed at all, He'd never lifted one finger to help Luke or any of the people Luke cared about.

He grabbed his jacket and pulled it on as he headed downstairs and out the back door. He needed to do something to work out some frustration and a ride was just what he needed. The ranch was pretty well locked down and the security alerts would come right to his cell phone, notifying him if something or someone set them off.

He walked to the stables. His grandfather's ranch manager, Ed Lance, had taught Luke to ride when he was eight. It was a skill he didn't use often, but he wanted to put it to work now.

Ed was in the horse barn cleaning when Luke entered. "What are you doing here?" Luke asked him. "Don't you have people to do that for you?" Ed had been with Harmon Ranch for close to thirty years and had worked his way up from stable boy to ranch manager. He was the last person Luke had expected to see cleaning the stalls.

"I do, but I enjoy taking care of the horses. I've been doing it for years. What are you doing out here?"

"Thought I'd take a ride."

Ed nodded. "I'll saddle Moose up for you. He belonged to your grandfather. I guess now he belongs to you boys."

"I'll do that," Luke insisted, pulling down the saddle and tack from the shelf. "I still remember how you taught me."

Ed grinned and watched Luke as he saddled the horse. "You do much riding these days?"

"Some. There was a stable a few miles from my apartment, but my job with the FBI was always so crazy. I never felt like it was the right time to buy my own horse."

"Well, I guess you own at least some of them now."

He was already stressed enough without the reminder that he had to make a decision about the ranch. When he'd arrived in town, his intention had been set. He was going to sell his share to one of his cousins as quickly as possible and get back out of here. Everything had changed the moment he'd discovered he had a daughter in town. Assuming he could find her and safely bring her home, he couldn't just leave town again if it meant leaving her behind, could he?

He hadn't even allowed his mind to consider those possibilities.

"He loved you, you know."

Luke glared at Ed. He liked the man, but Ed's staunch loyalty to Chet Harmon was something he'd never understood. "He had a strange way of showing it."

"He lost all of his sons. You four grandkids were all he had left. He was a broken and bitter man for a long time, but at least he found peace at the end."

"What do you mean?"

"A few months before he died, he found Jesus. He gave his life over to the Lord. He even finally allowed me to put that sign up."

Luke turned to see a plank of wood with a painted Bible verse hanging on the wall. *Hatred stirreth up strifes: but love covereth all sins. Proverbs 10:12.*

Luke groaned and led the horse outside, feeling like he was being hounded by God from all sides. Ed hurried after him. "He was different at the end, Luke. He tried to contact you. He wanted to apologize, but you wouldn't take his calls."

"I didn't accept his calls, Ed, because there was nothing he could have said or done that would have changed anything between us. He made his choices and I made mine."

Luke climbed onto Moose and turned him toward the field, pushing the horse into a gallop. He didn't need to hear how his grandfather had changed or how God had worked in his life. Too many terrible things had happened for any amount of redemption to make it right.

Ed's words had just confirmed it for him. Any god that would accept a man like Chet Harmon could never be on Luke's side. And what kind of love could cover the wrongs his grandfather and then Abby had committed against him?

This conversation had only added to his stress and he was looking forward to a nice, long ride to work out his restless energy and clear his mind. He couldn't allow matters of faith or past baggage to distract him from the matters at hand—finding his daughter and keeping Abby and Dustin safe while he did so.

* * *

The sun was up when Abby awoke the next morning. She darted awake, suddenly aware of how late it was. She had things to do, including deciding whether or not to send Dustin to school. She'd hoped to have that conversation with him this morning. Once that was decided, she wanted to go by the house and survey the damage in the daylight. Hopefully some things could be salvaged.

She reached for her phone and saw several text messages from both Luke and Dustin. The former had taken the latter to school, then headed to the police station to get an update on the investigation.

She sighed and dialed the number for the school. She wasn't surprised Dustin had chosen to go, but he had nothing with him. No books. No computer. Not even a backpack. Mrs. Jennings answered the call, and when Abby explained her concerns, she dismissed them.

"Abby, we're taking care of Dustin. Don't you worry. Ms. Porter and I are making sure Dustin has everything he needs. She even found him a spare computer to use for his assignments, and I let him use a backpack we had in the lost and found. He's fine. Now, you go rest and try not to worry about him."

Abby felt better after their conversation. A happy tear slid down her cheek as she realized this was why she'd come back here to Jessup instead of moving Kenzie and Dustin to Atlanta with her. People here stepped up to help each other. She was so used to doing things on her own and not allowing others to help her; however, she'd gotten a hard lesson on how badly things would go if she tried to do everything herself when it came to being a parent to these kids. Fortunately, once she'd realized she really couldn't do it all alone, everyone had been quick to step up and pitch in. This was what small-town life was all about and she was starting to embrace it.

She took her phone and went downstairs to the kitchen for coffee. Hannah, the housekeeper, was there cleaning. She was a woman of about sixty and, like most of the ranch's employees, had worked for Luke's grandfather for years. Abby remembered she was always a kind woman.

"Mornin'," Hannah said as Abby entered the kitchen. "Luke told me what happened to you last night. I'm so sorry to hear about your house."

"Thank you, Hannah. I plan to go over there this morning and take a look at the damage." She walked to the coffeepot and poured some into a mug.

"Let me make you some eggs. You'll need your strength today."

"No, thank you. I'm not hungry."

Hannah gave a big smile. "Not like that boy of yours. He ate two helpings of my home-made pancakes. I also packed him a lunch. I hope that's okay."

Abby felt herself tear up at the woman's kindness. "Yes, it is. Thank you for looking out for him. I wish he or Luke had awoken me before they left."

"They thought you needed your rest. That Dustin worries about you. So does Luke."

She knew Hannah was right, but it still surprised her. After all she'd put Luke through, it showed what a good man he was that he still worried about her safety and did what he could to protect her. It was a nice feeling having him looking out for her again. Realistically, she knew it probably wouldn't last once Kenzie was safe at home, but, for now, it felt like they were turning a page.

"I remember how inseparable you and Luke were when you were kids," Hannah continued. She gave Abby a smile. "I thought

I saw some of that old spark there too when he talked about you."

Abby felt her face warm at that implication. Yes, she was glad Luke was here, but so many things stood in the way of them ever having a romantic relationship again. She was sure once Kenzie was home and the danger had passed, Luke would have to face the anger he'd been putting to the side for the sake of focusing on the case. And he'd never been the kind of man who forgave easily. She knew that firsthand too, witnessing the grudge he still held against his grandfather.

"I'm sure you're just reading into things, Hannah. I'm afraid our relationship ended a long time ago." She took several sips of coffee, then carried her mug to the sink and rinsed it out. "I'm going to get dressed, then head over to the house."

Hannah looked disappointed at Abby shutting down her talk of romance, but she nodded. "Luke said to tell you he pulled a car around front for you to use today. The keys are in it. It belongs to the ranch, so there's no need for a rental."

So he'd taken care of her once again. She felt herself flush again. "Thank you, Hannah. It was good to see you again."

She hurried up the steps, showered and changed her clothes and was in the car heading toward her house within an hour.

In the daylight, it looked even worse than when she'd left it, and her heart sank. Half of her house was completely gone and the rest was charred black. Tears pressed against her eyes as she got out and dug through the rubble, hoping to find something to salvage.

She located some photo albums that had minimal damage and a few other odds and ends, but most of their belongings were utterly ruined. She loaded her few findings into the car. They would be starting from scratch. Everything was gone.

She closed the trunk, surprised to see her neighbor Trent McDade standing at the head of her car. "I saw you out here and wanted to see if there was anything we could do for you or Dustin."

She smiled. Another gesture of small-town friendliness. "Thank you, Trent. We're fine for now."

He glanced at the house. "This is unbelievable. I heard the police believe the fire was intentionally set?"

Abby nodded. "I saw someone throw a fire-bomb through the window, then run off. This happened because I won't stop trying to find Kenzie."

He shook his head and sighed. "What are you going to do, Abby?"

"What do you mean?"

"I mean, you still have Dustin to think about. You and he were both nearly killed two nights ago. Not to mention the incident with the train the previous morning. Aren't you worried about his safety?"

"Of course I'm worried about Dustin. I'll do whatever it takes to keep him safe, but I won't stop looking for Kenzie either. I won't sacrifice one to save the other."

"Even if it means you might lose them both?"

She stared at him as the force of his words hit her. If she lost both of them... Even the thought was unbearable. But she'd never forgive herself if she just gave up on Kenzie—and she had a feeling Dustin wouldn't forgive her either. At least now, at Luke's, Dustin would be safe from attacks.

"Thank you for your concern, Trent. I should go. It's getting late and I have to pick Dustin up from school."

She climbed into the car and drove away, but Trent's words echoed in her mind. It wasn't like there was an instruction manual for how to keep one kid safe while another had been abducted. She was doing the best she could, although even she had to admit that her best the past few days hadn't been so great.

She pulled up to the school and parked. The clock on the dash indicated she was a few minutes late. Dustin would be expecting her and she hated to make him wait, especially now when he was feeling extra vulnerable.

She glanced around but didn't see him right away. When she did, her heart stopped. She gripped the steering wheel as she recognized the slouching shoulders and the bright red tennis shoes he'd purchased last night. He was leaning into a car window and laughing. That might not bother her—in fact, it should have made her happy to see him laugh and smile after all they'd gone through—except that she spotted the person in the passenger seat of the car he was leaning into.

Tiffany Bell.

What was she doing even talking to a middle schooler? It was odd enough her hanging around with Kenzie, but Dustin was only a seventh grader. She had no business talking to him.

Abby cut the engine and hopped from the car. Her pulse pounded and fear settled in. "Dustin!"

He stood and turned to her, his face reddening. "Aunt Abby, what are you doing?"

"Get away from her." Her tone sounded frantic even to her own ears, but she couldn't help it. She had to get him away from Tiffany Bell as fast as possible.

Tiffany turned to look at her and flashed her a smug smile. The driver leaned across her and peeked out—Pete Lewis.

"We were only talking," Lewis said, as if trying to justify himself.

Abby grabbed Dustin's arm and pulled him back toward the car. She spun back around and looked at Tiffany and Lewis. "You stay away from him."

Lewis laughed. "You should keep a better eye on your kiddos, Abby. You've already lost one. I'd hate to see you lose another."

She guided Dustin back toward the car. "I don't want you speaking to either of those people."

He stopped and jerked his arm away. "I can't believe you embarrassed me that way. I was only talking to them. They seemed nice."

"They're not. Trust me. They're bad news."

He climbed into the passenger seat and slammed the door. "I don't need you picking my friends for me, Aunt Abby. I can decide who I want to hang out with."

She didn't like his tone and normally would have called him on it, but she had bigger concerns. She pulled on her seat belt, then started the engine and roared from the parking lot. "No, you can't. Not when you pick people like that. Don't you realize those two probably had a hand in abducting your sister?"

"They had nothing to do with Kenzie's disappearance. They were just telling me how sorry they were about her and how much they like her."

"They were toying with you, Dustin. And I believe that that man was driving one of the trucks that pushed us on the tracks—and might even have started the fire last night."

He folded his arms and his face hardened. "I was there—I know that you couldn't see anyone's faces. You don't know that it was him. You just don't want me to have any friends. I finally make some and you embarrass me."

He was quiet on the rest of the ride to the ranch and Abby didn't press him. He wasn't yet old enough to understand how the world worked, and he was so hungry for friends that a pretty girl smiling at him and an older guy chatting him up made him feel special.

Kenzie had fallen for it too. How many other kids had those two used that tactic on?

They reached the ranch and Dustin got out, slamming the car door and marching inside. By the time she'd followed him in, he'd darted up the stairs to his bedroom and slammed that door.

"What's going on with him?" Luke asked her.

"I went to pick him up from school and found Tiffany and Lewis getting a little too close for comfort with Dustin. They outright laughed at me, Luke. They said I'd better keep a better eye on Dustin before I lost him too. I dragged him away as fast as I could—which apparently embarrassed him."

His jaw clenched but he hugged her tightly. "You did the right thing getting him out of there."

"I was so scared when I saw him talking to them. I'm even more sure now that they know where Kenzie is. You didn't see how they taunted me." His embrace was warm and comforting. She knew she should pull away from him but she didn't want to. Finally, she forced herself to step back. She wiped a tear from her eye. "Do you think they were trying to lure Dustin in too? Do I need to be worried about his safety?"

Luke stared up the stairs. "I don't know. So far, it's only girls who have gone missing. Still, he should probably remain at the ranch as much as possible. I think they were probably just taunting you, but we can't be too careful."

"It won't matter if he won't ever speak to me again."

"I'll talk to him. Explain things. Sometimes a man-to-man talk is just what's needed."

She was suddenly very thankful this man had come back into her life. "Thank you, Luke."

She'd struggled with raising these kids for two years and all that time wishing she'd had someone to share the responsibilities with... someone like Luke.

Whoa, slow down, Abby.

They'd made a lot of progress in their relationship, but they weren't there yet. She wasn't entirely sure he'd ever be able to forgive her enough to start another romantic relationship with her. The most she could reasonably hope for now was a civil co-parenting situation with Kenzie. And if he could find it in his heart to be there for Dustin too, then she would be extra appreciative.

He owed her nothing and she owed him everything.

Yet she couldn't stop hoping.

Luke had told Dustin to make himself at home and the kid had done it. He'd plastered posters he'd gotten from friends at school on the wall of one of the spare bedrooms and strewn his few clothes everywhere. Luke couldn't help but chuckle at seeing the room. He was glad Dustin felt comfortable enough here at the ranch. Only, he wasn't in his room, so Luke went in search of him.

It had come easily to assure Abby that he would talk to Dustin. He remembered being a scared kid with nowhere and no one to turn to. And he did understand Dustin getting angry at Abby. It was so easy for a person to take out their frustrations on those they loved most, not least because they were safe targets. Dustin knew he could lash out at his aunt without worrying about her lashing back.

He slipped on his jacket and cowboy hat and walked down to the stables, not surprised when he found Dustin brushing one of the horses while Ed worked a few feet away at a safe but supervisory distance.

"He came down a little while ago and wanted to help, so I gave him a chore to do. I hope that's all right," Ed said.

"It's fine," Luke assured him. "I'll take over and make sure the horse is stalled, if you want to go."

He nodded, gathered his papers and walked out. "See you later, kid."

"'Bye, Ed." Dustin continued brushing but glanced at Luke. "I guess she sent you down here to talk to me."

Luke pulled off his jacket and draped it across a chair. He picked up a grooming brush and started on the other side. "Actually, I told her I would do it. It seemed like you were pretty upset about what happened."

He shrugged but didn't answer right away. When he did, his voice was low and embarrassed. "I don't have a lot of friends. It's usually just me and my best friend, Tony. Tiffany is one of the most popular girls in school and wanted to talk to me. I can't believe Aunt Abby overreacted that way. How am I ever going to show my face at that school again?"

"You can because your aunt didn't overreact, Dustin. Tiffany and that boyfriend of hers are definitely involved in what happened to Kenzie. I'm not saying they committed the abduction themselves, but they're involved. I believe they know where your sister is—and they're working with the people who are keeping her there, not letting her come home. You really need to stay away from them."

"Aunt Abby got to you too," Dustin grumbled, refusing to make eye contact.

"Did you forget what I do, Dustin? I'm an FBI agent. I see stuff like this all the time and I'm telling you those two are bad news. They're in this up to their eyeballs, and when I get some proof, I'm going to arrest them both. I don't want to see you get caught up in something because you're not listening to your gut."

At that, Dustin finally looked up at him. "What do you mean?"

"I mean, deep down somewhere, you know your aunt is right. You know Tiffany and Lewis are bad news. You knew it the moment they spoke to you. Did they ever do that before?"

The boy fought the truth for a moment, then shook his head. "No." His shoulders drooped and he looked crestfallen.

"You don't need those two to make you feel

special, Dustin. You're a great kid and some-times having that one friend is all you need."

"That's easy for you to say. I'll bet you were the most popular kid in school."

Luke laughed. "Well, then you'd be wrong. I was awkward and shy. I had one gift that earned me some popularity, and that was playing baseball, but I lost that when I blew my arm out."

"Still, you probably had a ton of friends."

"Nope, just one. Abby." He'd occasionally had his cousins and teammates to hang around with, but Abby had been his constant companion.

"Aunt Abby was your best friend?"

"We were tight. My life wasn't exactly easy."

Dustin rolled his eyes. "Oh yeah, I can tell. Growing up on this massive ranch must have been torture."

"Actually, I grew up in a one-room apart-ment six miles from here. I wasn't always allowed to come to the ranch because my grandfather couldn't get along with my mother. There were periods of peace between them when I could come and roam around, learn to ride and care for the horses. It was nice and I always wished it would stay that way, but it never did. The peace would end and they would go back to fighting and putting me in the middle, both of them trying to use me as a pawn to get their own ways."

Dustin stared at him. "What did you do?"

"I spent a lot of time hitting baseballs and running around town with your aunt. I did my best to stay under the radar until I was old enough to get away from them."

Dustin put up the grooming brush, looking thoughtful. "And I thought I had it bad after losing my parents. Kenzie and I both thought it would be terrible when Aunt Abby moved out here to take care of us. She wasn't around much when my parents were alive. We didn't know her all that well. But it wasn't terrible. I really like her. She's good to us."

"I know she loves you both."

He nodded. "It hasn't been easy for her either. Kenzie hasn't been easy. Even I know that."

"She's been hurting, that's all. It's understandable. You both lost so much and people grieve in their own ways."

Dustin removed the ropes that held the horse, then guided him into a stall and placed a blanket over him. It was obvious this wasn't his first time around horses. He locked the stall, then turned back to Luke.

"I'll apologize to her."

"I know she'd appreciate that. And I'll be proud of you too. It takes a real man to admit he made a mistake and to try to put things right." Dustin stood up a little straighter at that, clearly pleased to be referred to as a man. Hiding a smile, Luke dispensed one last piece of advice. "Dustin, don't judge your aunt too harshly. She's only trying to look out for you."

Dustin started to walk out of the barn but turned back to look at Luke. "Were you and Abby…? I mean, did you…? Was she your girlfriend?"

That question caught him off guard. "She was, but she was also my best friend," he told Dustin, but even that didn't do enough to encapsulate the relationship they'd shared. His best friend, his secret-keeper, the one he vented his frustrations to, his first kiss and first everything else.

She'd been his everything.

And she'd destroyed him by leaving him.

Back then, he'd naively believed that was the worst she could do to him, but he'd been so wrong.

Being with her now was bringing up all those old feelings toward her and he was struggling to keep them at bay. How could he love her again when he wasn't sure if he could ever forgive her?

And, more importantly, why did he even want to?

It was a question he struggled with every day, and he had yet to come up with the answer.

He had to keep his focus on the investigation, on finding Kenzie, not on his returning feelings for a woman who'd already shattered him.

Abby watched from the window as Dustin and Luke talked. It warmed her to see how good Luke was with him. He had a knack with kids and would make a great father.

Her face flushed at that thought. He would have made a great father fourteen years ago too, but she'd robbed him of that chance. If they could find Kenzie and bring her home, he might have another opportunity. If they didn't, he might never forgive Abby for robbing him the way she had.

Dustin approached the house. His shoulders were squarer and he walked with more confidence. He opened the door and spotted her staked out by the window.

"Are you okay?" she asked him.

He shrugged. "I guess so. I know you were right. I just didn't want to believe it. I thought they really liked me. I'm sorry I got mad at you."

She went to him and hugged him, loving it when he returned her hug.

"Luke said you were his girlfriend once. I like him, Aunt Abby. Why did you break up?"

She sucked in a breath. He was offering her an opportunity to share the truth with him but she couldn't. Not before she'd even told Kenzie about her parentage. "It's a long story."

"Well, I think you messed up. He's a nice guy." Dustin headed up the stairs and disappeared into his room.

Abby went back to the window. Luke was still outside and she felt the pull to go talk to him.

He was leaning against a post in the corral when she approached him. "Thank you for that. Dustin seems better after talking to you."

"He's a good kid."

"Yes, he is. I wish I could take credit for it, but he was raised right."

"Don't sell yourself short, Abby. You've been good to him. He told me so."

A swell of gratitude hit her. She'd tried

so hard to make a good life for these kids. She was glad to know that at least Dustin thought she'd done a good job. "He was the easy one," she admitted. "But I think their parents' deaths really hit Kenzie the hardest. It was so unexpected. One instant, they had a family, and the next, it was gone."

He sighed and stared out at the landscape. It was beautiful here.

"Somehow life never seems to turn out the way we expect it to." The cynicism in his voice troubled her. She understood his frustration. She'd caused a lot of it. She deserved his anger. But she hated to see him carrying the weight of it. She wished she could take some of that weight from his shoulders, but that wasn't possible—not unless he was willing to let it go.

He pulled a hand through his hair and groaned. "I thought I was going to leave town, marry you and have a baseball career. Nothing worked out the way I planned it. First, I lost you, then my shot at the pros. I finally found something I could feel good about with the FBI. Now that might be taken from me too."

He hadn't talked much about his time with the FBI or why he might not be returning to it. "Do you want to talk about it? Did something happen?"

He nodded and gripped his hands on the corral slats. "I lost someone. A team member, Michelle Simmons. She was young, only twenty-six and new to the agency. We were tracking a killer. When we raided his house, he knew he was cornered. He grabbed Michelle and used her as a shield, threatening to kill her."

"What happened?"

"I did what I was trained to do. I tried to de-escalate the situation. I tried to talk him down, but I knew he wasn't going to surrender. He'd done so many terrible things, hurt so many people. I've seen the type a hundred times before. No remorse. But I wanted to take him alive. I wanted his victims' families to be able to see him put on trial to get the justice he deserved. Plus, I wasn't sure I could take the shot without hurting Michelle. He was using her for cover and it was a risky shot. Only, while I was wrestling with all that, he slit Michelle's throat right in front of me."

Abby gasped at the horror of that situation. "That's awful. What did you do?"

"I shot him. Killed him. Now there's a big inquiry into Michelle's death. The agency is looking to place blame on someone, so they've chosen me. There's a formal hearing next month. If they decide I didn't act appropriately, I could lose my badge." He sighed and rubbed the back of his neck. "The truth is I'm not sure I want to go back even if they clear me, especially now. I was already thinking about leaving the agency, and the moment I found out about Kenzie, everything changed. How can I leave town knowing she's here? Knowing I'm needed here?"

She couldn't help but smile at the idea of Luke remaining in Jessup and being a father to Kenzie. For a moment, she allowed herself to dream about a future where she saw him regularly, maybe even renewed their relationship. She quickly pushed those thoughts away. Being a father to Kenzie didn't mean he'd want any kind of ongoing relationship with Abby.

"At least you won't have to worry about where you'll live, now that you've inherited part of the ranch."

She was trying to make him feel better but his shoulders sagged instead. "I've spent my entire life trying to get away from here, Abby. You know that. I love the space and the land and even the idea of caring for the livestock, but every inch of this place is tainted by the fights and the arguing and the demands my grandfather tried to place on me. I guess the truth is that there was always a part of me that loved being here. A part of me that envied Caleb at getting to live here. But that desire made me feel guilty. Like I was choosing my grandfather over my mom." He sighed and rubbed his face. "Nothing in my life has ever worked out the way I wanted it to. Everything I've ever loved has been taken from me." He shook his head. "God must really hate me."

Abby knew he had doubts when it came to matters of faith, but she knew too that God didn't hate him. He loved him and wanted the best for him. But how could she get Luke to see that?

"I don't know why you've lost so much, Luke, but God doesn't hate you. He's a generous and loving God. He's given me a second chance. I certainly never believed I deserved it after the bad decisions I made that affected everyone's lives—mine, yours, my sister's, Kenzie's. Okay, yes, maybe you have lost a lot, but look at all you've gained. This ranch, a second chance with your daughter."

"If we can find her."

"We'll find her. I believe in you, Luke. I have no choice but to believe in you."

She wanted so much to take away his pain, to offer him the same forgiveness she'd found through Jesus Christ, but he was so defeated and so angry. Could God reach his bitter heart?

He could. If He could reach past her selfishness, He could reach past Luke's bitter resentment as well.

"Maybe this is your second chance."

He turned to look at her and his eyes were filled with measured hope. He reached out and pushed a strand of hair from her face. She stared up at him and felt a desire to crawl into his embrace, bury her head against his shoulder and not come out until Kenzie was home safe. He'd always been her protector. Even when they were kids, he was the one she'd turned to. She'd lost a tremendous amount when she'd pushed him away and she regretted it. She had so many regrets.

But she couldn't focus on them. They were in the past and she couldn't do anything about them. This was now and she could only act based on what was happening today. She'd needed Luke again and he'd suddenly appeared. That wasn't a coincidence. God had promised to restore to her what the locusts had eaten. She'd clung to that passage in Joel when she'd first discovered her faith. Now she was beginning to see the fruition of that promise. He'd restored her relationship with her daughter, giving her another chance to be a parent. Now he'd brought Luke Harmon back into her life.

"Is a second chance even really possible?" he asked, his voice cracking with emotion.

He stroked her cheek, his eyes moving to her lips. She felt him tense and the connection between them electrified.

She could tell that he wanted to kiss her, and she welcomed it. She leaned into him and lifted her head, and he claimed her lips.

For a moment, time stood still. They were back to fifteen years ago. Heady with love and dreaming of a future together.

He broke off the kiss and stared at her. His breathing was rushed and heavy, and it was clear that the kiss had affected him strongly, but he shook his head and his expression changed. He was backing away, emotionally and physically.

She grabbed his shirt and tried to pull him back to her dream world. "It's okay," she told him.

"No, it's not," he whispered back, his tone full of pain and regret. He reached for her hands and held them as he struggled to compose himself. She saw the conflict waging in his expression. "I can't deny I'm still attracted to you, Abby, but we're not kids anymore. It can never be like it was between us. Too much has happened."

She gulped, feeling like he was about to shatter her hopefulness.

"When you first told me about Kenzie, I was so angry at you. I thought I would never be able to forgive you for what you did."

"And now?"

"And now I just don't know. I can't even process what I'm feeling. I have to keep my focus on finding my daughter and dealing with that new reality before I can even begin to think about you and me."

She understood the swirling emotions he must be feeling. She was feeling them herself and she had less to process than he did. But she was hopeful there might be a chance that he could forgive her, look past old wounds and move on to a future together. After all, the attraction was still there. He obviously still cared for her and wanted to move past this.

Yet he was right. Finding Kenzie had to be their top priority.

She touched her lips, the feel of his embrace still making them tingle with delight. She touched his face, then gave him a reaffirming smile. "I understand. I know you don't believe, Luke, but I'm praying that one day soon, after our daughter is home and safe, that you'll be able to find it in your heart to forgive me. I know it seems like a huge obstacle, but I also know that, with God, all things are possible."

"I just need some time," he told her. "Since the moment I arrived back in Jessup, my life has been spinning out of control. The only way I'm getting through it is to take it one thing at a time. For now, all I can focus on is finding my daughter—our daughter—and bringing her home."

She understood that and agreed. For now, she would give him the space he needed to figure things out. She just hoped that second chance she'd been praying for would find its way to reality.

EIGHT

Luke needed to get to the police station, but he felt better about leaving Abby and Dustin knowing they were at the ranch. They'd be safe there while he dived back into the case. Caleb and his team were working around the clock interviewing the families of the other missing girls and looking for a pattern between them all, but Luke felt better when he was involved in the process.

He met with Caleb to get an update on all they were doing. He couldn't find any fault in his cousin's investigative procedures and his staff were dedicated and skilled. Luke was glad to be working with such an efficient group.

Caleb finished giving him the lowdown on where they were, then gave Luke a knowing look. "How are Abby and Dustin? Are they settling into the ranch?"

"They're okay. Dustin had a little drama at school today. Abby caught Tiffany and Lewis talking to him in the parking lot. I doubt he'll be going back to school for a while after that."

"They didn't hurt him, did they?"

"No. I think they were just trying to get a rise out of Abby." He laughed, recalling her determined look when she'd returned home. "I'm sure she gave them both an earful. She's a pistol."

Caleb grinned. "You two seem to be getting along better."

He nodded. He couldn't deny it. Something had definitely changed between them, especially after that kiss by the barn. He hadn't meant to do it, but it had felt so right to hold her and kiss her again.

That was until he'd come to his senses.

"Looks like you're on your way to forgiving her, then?"

He shrugged. "I don't know. On one hand, how can I blame her? We were just kids. Yes, she should have come to me first, but I can understand why the girl she was back then— determined to make a name for herself, terrified of failure—would feel like she didn't have any other choice. Not to mention I'm not sure we would be anywhere different than we are now. Giving the baby to Danielle and Matt really was the best choice, so not much would have changed." Except that he would have known all these years he'd had a daughter.

He couldn't dwell on that. He had to put the past in the past if he hoped to have any sort of future. Was he really imagining a future with Abby? He realized he might be. He could see how she was trying to make up for the mistakes she'd made. Somehow, he felt the need to forgive her. He just couldn't make himself let go of all that anger and resentment toward her. Until he could find a way to work through that, there could never be a future for them as a family.

He realized that, in spite of himself, he was already thinking of a future with her and Dustin and Kenzie. His heart gripped at that thought. First, he had to find his daughter. Their leads were coming up dry. A trafficking ring was operating right under their noses and Luke couldn't find a single scrap of a lead to bring the criminals to justice.

Some FBI agent he was.

Maybe the agency was right. Maybe it was time for him to retire.

Caleb shot him a look, then grinned.

"You're already head over heels, aren't you? I knew you couldn't resist Abby for too long. Not after how mesmerized you used to be about her."

"I'm not sure how I feel." He wasn't ready yet to call it love. He wasn't ready to go that far. Too much still remained between them.

"I told Abby that, until we find Kenzie, I can't make any decisions about us."

"Why do you keep trying to talk yourself out of being in love?" Caleb asked him. "It's obvious you're wild about Abby. You care about Dustin and I know you're going to be a great dad to Kenzie. What's your deal?"

His cousin didn't understand how many times he'd seen his future go up in smoke. Just when he'd thought his life was moving in the right direction, everything had fallen apart every time. He sighed and rubbed his face. "I can see a future stretching out before me and I want it, Caleb, but I've been burned too many times. Every time I think I'm finally getting all I've ever wanted, it gets snatched out from under me. I'm not sure I could stand it if that happens again. And it might. What if we can't find Kenzie? What would that do to Abby's and my relationship? I'm not sure we could come back from that."

"First of all, that's not going to happen. We're going to find her. Secondly, you can't survive a relationship you've never had. Love is a risk, Luke, but it's one you have to be willing to take."

He knew his cousin was right, but avoiding that risk was the one sure way to make sure his heart would never be crushed again. And if they never brought Kenzie home, would he ever be able to truly forgive Abby?

It was a question he'd decided not to confront. At least, not yet.

"I think I'll get in touch with Amy and see if the FBI task force has come across anything that might help us."

Caleb left and he pulled up the video conference app on his phone. He dialed her number and she answered right away. "How's it going, Luke?"

"Not great," he admitted. "I was hoping you might have something for me."

"I'm sorry. I don't have anything new to offer. Have you found any commonalities between the missing girls?" Amy asked him.

"Not yet. They're all from different economic backgrounds and from different parts of the county."

"I looked through the information you sent

me about your prime suspect, Pete Lewis. I have to say I agree with you that he seems unlikely to have orchestrated a trafficking ring of this size. If he's involved, he has to be answering to someone."

Luke agreed with that assessment, but it didn't help them move the case along. He rubbed a hand over his face and sighed. "We're getting nowhere, Amy. How do we find these girls?"

"I wrote a computer program to search through the landowner rolls for your county. I'm comparing them against known traffickers. I also updated the task force with the photographs you sent me of the missing girls, including Kenzie's. We constantly monitor dark-web sites that try to auction off women, and we're on alert for any possible matches to these photos. But until we can find a connection between them, I'm afraid all we can do is wait."

He thanked her for her help, then clicked off the call. He leaned back in his seat. Waiting wasn't his strong suit. Kenzie had already been missing for several days and each day it grew less likely they would find her.

He turned back to the evidence board where Caleb's team had put up pictures of all the missing girls. They ranged in age from twelve to twenty. Different ages. Different hair colors. Different body types. From what he could tell from the interviews and reports, none of them were friends or attended the same church. The only connection between this group of missing teens seemed to be that they all attended school in the county.

Abby believed Kenzie had been groomed by Tiffany, an older girl with charm, looks and popularity. If that was the case, there should a person serving a similar function in each school. But no way an organized ring would allow these girls to operate in a school setting without some kind of supervision. What if they called out for help or approached a teacher about the life they were trapped in? Someone had to be watching them. It wasn't Lewis either. He wasn't a student and wouldn't be allowed in the school building when classes were in session. A teacher made sense, but how would they get a teacher in their organization at every school in the county?

He pulled up the teacher lists for East Lake, then for the other schools. Was it possible there was a teacher who moved from school to school? A substitute wouldn't have the kind of access needed on a regular basis, so it had to be someone with a more permanent commitment. A librarian or a nurse or a…

His eye caught on a name common to each school.

Someone who moved throughout the system without being noticed. Someone who could possibly lead them to the person in charge and to the whereabouts of his daughter.

He hurried to tell his cousin about what he'd found.

If he was right, this could be the break they'd been waiting for.

Abby felt helpless. She was stuck at home—well, stuck at Luke's home—with no way to look for Kenzie. Her attempts to find her had failed and her body was suffering the effects of the attacks against her.

But she couldn't give up. She'd couldn't stop searching for Kenzie…and she wouldn't. She would never give up on her.

Dustin had already eaten and gone up to his room. It was too early for him to go to sleep, but he would occupy himself with a movie or with games on his phone until bedtime—which was a bit later than usual since he wouldn't be getting up early for school.

She'd decided after seeing him with Tiffany and Pete Lewis that school was no longer a safe place for him. He wasn't going back as long as those two were still roaming free.

She fixed herself a cup of tea and curled up on the couch. She pulled up social media on her laptop and clicked on Tiffany's profile. She knew she shouldn't do it, but she couldn't help herself. This young woman was the key to finding her daughter. Abby believed it more now than she ever had.

She scrolled through past posts. It was mostly a bunch of attention-seeking nonsense that made Abby wonder if her parents knew how much she was putting out there for the world to see. Did she even have parents? She was seventeen and dating an older man. It was possible her parents had no clue what was going on in her life.

Like you had no clue with Kenzie.

The thought stung her but it was the truth. Kenzie had dropped her best friend, Ashley, for a more popular friend, hung out at the auto repair shop of a much older man and searched online for her biological father, all without Abby's knowledge. What kind of parent did that make her?

She stopped scrolling through Tiffany's

posts when a photograph caught her eye. In it, Tiffany was standing on the porch of an abandoned restaurant. Abby recognized the ornate white trim of the old porch. One of the first stories she'd done when she'd returned to town was to report on the closing of the long-established restaurant Hal's Homestyle Barbeque. It had been a staple in the town for forty years until the owner, Hal, died. Even now, over a year later, his house and restaurant remained in limbo while his family fought over control of the properties.

She glanced at the date on the photo, certain it must be an old picture from before the place shut down, but it was dated only a few days ago. As further proof, the shirt she was wearing was one the school had offered recently for sale. What would Tiffany have been doing at a place like that?

She examined the photo more closely and spotted something else. In one image, Tiffany's hair was pushed back and she was wearing a pair of sunflower earrings. Kenzie had a pair just like them that had been a gift from her mother. She never took them off and she'd been wearing them the day she was abducted.

Horror raced through Abby. Was Tiffany wearing Kenzie's earrings?

Her logical mind tried to dismiss that thinking. Kenzie wasn't the only girl in town who had sunflower earrings, surely, and if Danielle had bought them locally, then it was very possible that plenty of people had identical pairs, but it seemed an awfully big coincidence to her.

She grabbed her cell phone and called Luke. This photo might not be enough proof to get a warrant to search Tiffany's house, but they should at least check out this restaurant and find out what the teenager was doing hanging around there.

"Abby, I'm going to have to call you back," Luke said immediately after answering her call. "I'm right in the middle of something."

"Wait, Luke. This is important."

His tone changed to one of urgency. "What is it? Has something happened?"

"I was looking at Tiffany's social media page and there's a picture of her wearing a pair of earrings that look just like Kenzie's. And the picture was taken at this restaurant that has been closed down for over a year, Hal's Homestyle Barbeque. I know the building was in some kind of real-estate limbo."

He sighed, obviously not finding her discoveries important enough. "Abby, lots of people have matching earrings. That's hardly a smoking gun."

"But the restaurant. We should go check it out. This could be a place where they're holding the girls."

"Text me the name. I'll check it out tomorrow if we still need to. We're interviewing someone right now that might be able to tell us everything about who is behind this ring."

"Who?"

"Shyla Porter."

"The school counselor?" Abby remembered the way she'd blocked them from getting answers from Tiffany.

"She's the only school employee who goes around the county to every school. So far, I can place her with access to each of the missing girls."

Abby was stunned but excited about this new development. "Has she told you where Kenzie is yet?"

"Not yet, but I'm confident we'll get answers from her soon. We're digging into her finances and phone records as well. I'll call you later, okay?"

"Okay." She ended the call, thankful that Luke had made some progress. That was good news indeed.

It all made sense. Someone like Shyla Porter had access to girls at every school in the county. She would be able to recruit girls to help her groom and lure others into their ring and still be able to keep an eye on each one of them.

Finally, answers. *Thank You, God.*

She closed her computer and set it aside. No use stalking Tiffany's page anymore. If the girl was involved, Ms. Porter would eventually tell them. Luke would get the truth from her and finally uncover the leader of the ring and the location where they were keeping the girls.

She tried to concentrate on other things as she waited anxiously for Luke's call, but her mind kept going back to that photograph and those sunflower earrings. If those did belong to Kenzie, it meant that Tiffany had seen her since the abduction.

She glanced at her phone again. Still no call or text from Luke. Were they still drilling the counselor for answers? And how long would this questioning take? She knew from her investigative days that police procedures moved slowly and interrogations could go on for hours.

It wouldn't hurt to check out the abandoned

building and confirm for herself that no one was squatting there. In fact, she would be saving Luke a step because he wouldn't have to do it himself. He'd seemed pretty dismissive of the idea, which meant that he clearly didn't think it would be dangerous.

She grabbed her keys before she changed her mind. She should call him or text him to let him know where she was going and what she was doing, but what was that old saying? Better to ask for forgiveness than permission.

She was in the car and at the end of the lane before she even gave it a second thought. She was only going to do a drive-by and see if the lights were on. If they were, she would phone Luke. If they weren't, she would be back at the ranch before Luke even knew she'd been gone.

So far, Shyla Porter had been tight-lipped since Luke and Caleb had brought her in for questioning.

They were still waiting on the warrant to come through for her cell phone records and financials, but, until then, Luke was plying her with questions, looking for any opening to get her talking about her involvement in this trafficking ring.

"We know you are involved in this, Shyla. Tell us what we need to know and you'll go a long way toward helping yourself out of this mess. Tell us where they're holding the girls. Otherwise, you could be going to jail for a very long time."

She clasped her fingers together and stared at Luke. "I don't know what you're talking about. I'm not involved in anything."

"You're the only employee that goes to every school in the district, and I have school records that prove you counseled each one of the missing girls."

"Of course I did. As well as dozens more. I'm a school counselor. That's my job. It's not my fault the school district won't pony up more money for another counselor."

Luke sighed. She might be able to deny her involvement for now, but once those warrants came through and they dug into her life, it would be over for her.

He pulled out a folder and decided to take another approach when his cell phone dinged. He slipped it from his pocket and saw an alert from the GPS on one of the ranch's vehicles. He'd activated them in case something happened to Abby again while she was driving. Right now, it alerted him to movement. He clicked on the

GPS and realized the car was headed to the east side of town, where Hal's Homestyle Barbeque Restaurant had once been located.

Anger bit through him. What was she thinking going there alone?

He gathered his files, got up and walked out of the interrogation room. He dialed her number, but after several rings, the call went to voice mail.

Great. Now she was avoiding his calls.

He found Caleb and let him know he was heading out. "I have to go. Abby might be in trouble."

"Do you need backup?" Caleb asked.

"I'll call if I do." He highly doubted that anything was going on there, but it was reckless of her to leave the safety of the ranch to go check.

Still, he turned on his sirens and sped across town. Even if there wasn't a trafficking ring operating out of Hal's old building, anyone could be squatting there and might pose a threat to her.

Thankfully, traffic was light and he caught up to her just a block away from the building. He sped past her, cut her off, then forced her to stop the car. He slammed the car into Park, then hopped out to confront her.

She got out of the car too. "Why did you do that?"

"What were you thinking coming here by yourself, Abby?" All his anger poured out of him. She'd taken an unnecessary risk and put her life in danger.

"I just want to check out the building. I wasn't going to get out of my car. How did you even know I was here?"

"All the cars at the ranch have GPS. I activated them in case of an emergency."

Her eyes widened and her mouth fell open. "You mean you were tracking me? How dare you?"

"How dare *I*? I'm not the one sneaking around trying to get herself killed or worse. Did you even think about Dustin and what would happen to him if he lost you too, Abby? Or me?"

"I was thinking about finding Kenzie."

"I told you I was working on it, that I'd check this place out tomorrow, but that wasn't good enough for you, was it? You never trusted me."

She flinched at that, finally looking a little apologetic. "I do trust you, Luke."

"No, you don't. You never have. You didn't trust me enough to tell me about the baby in the first place. You just made the decision and cut me out. And you don't trust me enough now to truly let me into your life, Abby."

A tear slid down her face. "That's not true. I do trust you. I've never trusted anyone in my life as much as I trust you." He could tell from her expression that she believed what she was saying to him, but it was her own behavior that told him where things really stood. She couldn't surrender her own will enough to ever trust another person.

And he could never build a life with someone who didn't trust him. Or who he couldn't trust.

It was time to stop thinking about his pie-in-the-sky dreams of having a family with this woman. He needed to find his daughter, forge a relationship with Kenzie, but move on with his life on the romance front.

He pulled his gun from his holster. "Let's go."

"What are you doing?"

"You wanted to check out this building, so let's go check it out. Stay behind me."

He walked down the street toward an empty building with the Hal's sign still hanging above the door. He stepped onto the porch, then tried the door handle. It was unlocked. He took out his flashlight and stepped inside, shining his light over the interior.

No one jumped out at them and he heard no sounds of people. He tried the lights but nothing happened when he flipped the switch. No electricity meant it was unlikely anyone had been here. To appease her, he searched the old dining room, bathrooms and kitchen but saw no one and no evidence that anyone had been inside in quite a while. The place was dark and empty.

He holstered his gun as he walked out, making sure the door was closed behind them so not to invite squatters. He headed back to his car and Abby followed.

"I really thought someone would be here. But the earrings Tiffany was wearing in the picture, Luke. Those were definitely Kenzie's earrings. I'm sure of it."

He rubbed his hands over his face. She wouldn't even give up in the face of being proved wrong.

He walked to her car door and opened it for her. "Go home, Abby."

She stared at him, her mouth agape at his command. "Why are you acting this way?"

"You heard me. I have to get back to the police station, where we're doing some actual investigating. I have a viable suspect in the interrogation room, so I don't have time to chase after you and pluck you out of harm's way at every turn. I'm working to find my daughter."

She folded her arms. "So am I."

That was the final straw. "No, what you're doing is wasting both of our time. You're not a cop, Abby, so go home before I arrest you for interfering with an investigation."

He left her standing there with her door open and climbed into his car. After a moment, she got into her car too and drove off.

He headed back to the station to finish questioning Shyla Porter. The sooner his daughter was found, the sooner they could all get on with their lives.

Abby pulled to the side of the road as tears threatened to overcome her. She couldn't stop thinking about her fight with Luke. Not just the humiliating end, where he'd scolded her for wasting his time, but the heartbreaking thing she'd said earlier, when he'd asserted that she didn't trust him.

She trusted him more than she'd ever trusted anyone in her life…yet he was right. She hadn't trusted him enough to let him do what he was trained to do and investigate. She'd tried over and over to take matters into her own hands.

She'd thought her determination made her strong, but she was quickly realizing how weak it had made her. She'd pushed away perhaps the one man who could help her, the man she believed God had sent to help her. And, if she couldn't give up control and trust Luke, in a way, she realized she wasn't trusting God either.

She dug through her purse for a tissue, then dabbed at her eyes. She didn't want to be this person. It was someone she thought she'd left behind a long time ago—the obsessive, ambitious, controlling woman who never considered the feelings of others. That was the woman who'd chosen her career over her baby daughter.

She felt ill at the idea of turning back into her again.

She stared out at the deserted street. The stores were closed for the night but the streetlamps still shone and the bright traffic lights cast an eerie glow over the area. She'd run from this town and from motherhood fifteen years ago. She hadn't realized at the time what a blessing this town and her family had been. It had taken nearly losing them all to wake her up, but she, finally, accepted that she belonged here in Jessup. She belonged to Kenzie and Dustin.

And she loved it.

Yet she'd known for a while that something else was missing in her life. Something else she'd tossed away fifteen years ago. Luke.

And here was God once again giving her a second chance that she'd blown again.

She picked up her cell phone and dialed his number. It went straight to voice mail. Now he wasn't even accepting her calls. After the way she'd ignored his call earlier, she knew she deserved it. What she had to say couldn't wait any longer, so she listened for the beep, then spilled her heart out to him. "Luke, I know you probably don't want to hear from me again, but I wanted to tell you how sorry I am that I made you feel like I didn't trust you. There's no one in my life I trust more. I believe God sent you to me for a second chance but I blew that. I know that I hurt you. That was the last thing I wanted to do." She sniffed back tears that were streaming down her face. She was hesitating, still fearful and holding back from him.

Tell him what you want to say, Abby.

"I love you, Luke. I've loved you for as long as I can remember. I know I've messed up and you might not be able to forgive me, but—"

The roar of a loud engine grabbed her attention, making her pause in the middle of her confession. Another car pulled up beside her, too close for comfort. Behind her the engine of a big truck thundered. She glanced into the rearview mirror and saw it, startling at the noise as the driver revved his accelerator. When she jumped, she accidentally dropped the phone at her feet.

The car beside her didn't move, but she couldn't see the occupants through the dark, tinted windows. Hairs on the back of her neck stood up. Everything felt wrong about this situation. She tried to regulate her breathing, to keep panic at bay, but she couldn't stop her stomach from turning somersaults. She had a bad feeling about this. A very bad feeling.

Her pulse kicked up as the window of the car beside her began to lower and Pete Lewis's face came into view. She struggled not to react. She couldn't let Lewis see how frightened she was. He wanted to see her fear, but she wasn't going to give him that satisfaction.

This was the man she was sure had taken

Kenzie. This was the man who had pushed her and Dustin onto the train tracks and set fire to their house.

She wouldn't put anything past him. And she was not going to become another one of his victims.

She slammed her foot against the accelerator and rushed from the curb and through the red light. The vehicles followed, speeding up to pass her. They easily overpowered hers.

She hunched down to try to find her cell phone. She had to call for help. The car swerved, nearly running off the road as she searched. She jerked it back onto the asphalt. Laughter roared from the open windows of the other vehicles. They were enjoying toying with her.

She gave up on the phone. Wherever it was, it was out of her reach and she needed to keep her eyes on the road.

Dread sank through her. She couldn't get away from them. Lewis and his friends could easily outdrive her, and without Luke to come to her rescue, she was a sitting duck.

But she would fight them tooth and nail. She would make sure it wasn't easy for them.

It didn't take Lewis long to get tired of playing with her. His car pulled up in front of her and cut her off, sending her to the side of the road. The other truck pulled up behind her, blocking her in.

This was it. She was trapped.

She dumped her purse out on the passenger seat. She searched for something, anything, to fight back with. She found nothing. She searched for the phone again, but it was lost somewhere beneath the seats, jostled probably as she sped away from her assailants.

The car door opened on the silver sedan and Lewis headed toward Abby. She took a deep breath. This was the moment of truth.

She locked the door but he had come prepared. He nodded at someone behind her and she turned to see a man with a crowbar at the passenger-side window. He smashed the glass, leaned in and disengaged the locks.

Lewis pulled open her door and slid into the seat, shoving her over the middle console as she scrambled to the other side of the car. The man who'd smashed the window slid into the passenger seat. She was trapped between them.

Lewis gave her a wicked smile that made her want to lash out at him.

"What—what do you want?"

He reached out and stroked her cheek with

his finger. She shuddered at the touch. "Don't you worry, Abby. We're not going to hurt you. The boss wants to have a word."

The boss? Was she finally going to meet the leader behind all this? The person responsible for giving the order to abduct her daughter? "Who is this boss? Does he know where Kenzie is?"

"You'll find out soon enough."

Suddenly a hand went over her face. Some kind of cloth was pressed against her mouth and nose, coated with a heady scent that sent her mind spinning.

They were knocking her out. She wasn't even going to get to see where she was heading.

The last thing she remembered before losing consciousness was being dragged from the car.

NINE

Luke eyed the voice mail notification on his phone.

He could see it was from Abby but he wasn't so sure he was ready to hear it.

He hadn't meant to be so harsh with her, but he was just so frustrated with her lack of willingness to trust him.

It was clear to him now that they'd never be able to make a romantic relationship work. He needed to move on from his growing feelings for Abby, no matter how much it hurt.

His phone rang and he glanced at the screen. Dustin. Odd.

"Do you know where Aunt Abby is?" the kid asked when Luke answered. "I can't find her anywhere. I came down to say good-night and she's not here. She didn't leave a note and she's not answering her phone."

Luke straightened in his seat. He'd left

Abby over two hours ago. She should have been home long before now.

The panic in Dustin's voice was understandable, but it kicked Luke's pulse up a notch with worry. "She ran an errand earlier, but she should have made it home by now," Luke answered. "Let me check and I'll call you back."

He didn't want to worry the kid, but he didn't like this. Why wasn't she home? And, more importantly, why not answer her phone? That didn't sit right with Luke. Abby might ignore Luke's calls, but she'd never do that to Dustin. She took her commitment to those kids seriously. He'd seen it for himself. If she wasn't there for Dustin, then something was wrong. Something had kept her from getting home.

He dialed her number, but the call went straight to voice mail. "Abby, call me as soon as you get this. Dustin is worried about you." He hesitated only a moment before continuing. "I am too."

He ended the call, then pulled up the GPS app on his phone and searched for her car. It was sitting on Old Canyon Road, at least three miles in the opposite direction of the ranch. And it was sitting still. It might have had mechanical trouble, but if that was the case, why hadn't she called for help?

He glanced at the voice mail notification. Maybe she had and he'd been too stubborn to answer.

He kicked himself, then pressed the icon to play the voice mail message.

Abby's voice filled the room and Luke smiled, relieved when she apologized instead of asking for help. He continued to listen, her words spinning their way into his heart. And when she told him she loved him, his heart swelled.

He was having such a hard time with this because he loved her too. He'd never stopped. He just didn't know whether the affection he felt for her would be enough for them to overcome the trust issues they both had.

His head jerked up at the sound of her screaming and what sounded like glass shattering.

He listened for several horrible seconds as she cried out for help before the call ended.

His heart hammered. He grabbed his keys and hollered for Caleb. "Something has happened to Abby. I think someone took her. Her car is parked on the side of Old Canyon Road. I'm heading there now."

Caleb nodded. "I have a patrol that's close. I'll send them, then meet you there."

He climbed into his SUV and shoved the key in the ignition. His hands were shaking with fear and he could hardly catch his breath. He couldn't stand hearing her tell him she loved him and then screaming in fear. It didn't matter what he'd told her earlier or even what he'd tried to tell himself. He loved her too. He'd never stopped loving her and it wasn't a feeling he could change or will away.

He gripped the steering wheel as he drove, his mind creating all sorts of terrible scenarios that he struggled to suppress.

His heart clenched as he spotted blue lights in the distance, then another vehicle that was pulled to the side of the road. Abby's car. His pulse quickened.

He steered to the side behind the patrol car, slammed the SUV into Park, then hopped out.

One of the two officers at the scene approached him. "We just arrived a few minutes ago. It was like this when we found it."

The car doors were opened on both sides. One had the glass window busted out of it. He felt the engine. It was cold. This car had been sitting here for a while. The assault he'd heard on his voice mail had been happening while he was too stubborn to answer her call.

"My partner is checking the area."

Off the highway was a patch of woods. It was possible she'd run in and hidden, but he doubted they would find her there. Still, he held on to hope.

"Abby!" He shouted for her, but there was no response and no movement in the brush. He hurried up the road and scanned the area. There was no sign of her.

The keys were still in the ignition. He grabbed them and walked around to the back of the car. His gut clenched as he approached the trunk. No sounds were coming from inside, so if she was there, she was either unconscious or dead. He didn't want to know but he had to look.

He took a deep breath and braced himself as he turned the key and opened the trunk.

His knees nearly buckled under him with relief when it was empty.

But that only meant one thing. They'd taken her. They'd taken Abby.

He pulled out his phone and dialed his cousin. "Her car's been abandoned on the side of the road. She's not here. Can you send a team out to check the car and tow it back to the station? I want the full forensic workup on it. It looks like there might have been a struggle here."

Normally he might give a list of all the things he wanted them to look for, but he couldn't even think about that right now. First, he had to go back to the ranch to talk to Dustin and reassure the boy that his aunt was going to be fine. He had no idea how he was going to do that when he wasn't sure it was true. But the kid deserved as much comfort as Luke was able to provide.

He hopped back into his SUV and headed for the ranch. Dustin was on the front porch when he arrived. He stood when Luke pulled up. His shoulders were tight and his jaw clenched. He was one big ball of nerves and the news Luke had wasn't going to make it any better.

"What happened? Where's Aunt Abby? I tried to call her phone and she didn't answer. She never has her phone off. She's never not answered me before."

Luke knew at that moment that he wouldn't lie to the kid. He deserved the truth. Yes, he would worry, but he could worry right alongside everyone else. "Honestly, Dustin, I don't know what's happened to Abby. I found her car abandoned on the outskirts of town. She wasn't there, but it looks like a struggle took place." He didn't tell him about what he'd heard on the voice mail message. It would just upset him further.

Dustin's body tensed even more, which Luke wouldn't have believed possible. He looked like he wanted to ask a question but was terrified to. Finally, he found his voice. "What—what do you think happened to her? Was it them? The same people that took Kenzie?"

"Maybe. I don't know. But I am going to find out."

He wasn't trying to give Dustin false reassurance. He meant what he said. He was going to find Abby, no matter where she was. And he was going to find Kenzie too.

He was going to bring them both home, where they belonged.

The first thing Abby was aware of was the stench surrounding her. Next, she noticed that her head felt like it was weighted down and her throat was dry and scratchy. She pulled open her eyes to try to figure out what was going on but her eyelids were heavy. Her muscles ached and she wondered for a moment what had happened to her.

Then it all came rushing back to her.

Lewis and his friends had chased her down, broken into her car and pressed a rag over her face. Whatever lingering effects she was feeling were from whatever had been on that rag.

She forced her eyes open and looked around. She was lying on a mattress in a small room. Someone was sitting beside her, her arms wrapped around her knees as she rocked back and forth. Abby recognized that stance and that silhouette.

"Kenzie?" Her voice was low and it hurt her to even speak those words, but the girl turned when she spoke.

She moved to hover over Abby, her wide-eyed expression full of concern. It was her eyes that Abby noticed first. Bright and blue.

Just like her father's.

"Aunt Abby? Are you okay?"

Seeing Kenzie sent a rush of adrenaline and happiness through her. She sat up and pulled her into a hug.

The girl clung to her. "I was so worried," she said. "When they brought you in unconscious, I was so worried you were dead. You wouldn't wake up."

"They drugged me with something, but I'm better now." She held Kenzie's face in her hands and her heart swelled with relief and love for this girl. She'd feared she might never see her face again. "Oh, Kenzie, I'm so glad to see you." She gave the girl a once-over. She was dressed in sweats and a tank top. Her hair was unwashed and stringy looking, her face and arms bruised and her lip busted, but she looked to be unharmed otherwise. "What about you? Are you okay? Did they hurt you?"

She shook her head, despite the busted lip she sported. "I'm okay. Just really scared, Aunt Abby."

Abby gathered her into another hug. She was never going to let her out of her sight again. "Everything is going to be okay," she assured her. "We're going to be okay."

Kenzie's lips trembled. "This is all my fault. I did this."

"What are you talking about?"

"I was looking for my real father. I met this guy online and started talking to him. He said he was my father, but I knew he wasn't. I knew he was lying the moment I saw him."

Abby sucked in a breath. Kenzie didn't know the truth that Luke was her father. "How did you know, Kenzie?"

"I'd seen him before with my friend Tiffany. I knew what they were up to and I told them I was going to tell someone what they were doing. She'd tried to get me to join in their parties, but I didn't want anything to do with it."

"Their parties?"

Kenzie bit her lip, then pushed a strand of hair behind her ear. "Sex parties. Tiffany befriends different girls, then gets them involved. She tried to lure me in, but I didn't want any part of it. She took me to this man's house, and when I realized what was happening, I ran." Tears streamed down her face. "It was that same man that claimed he was my father, so I knew it was a lie."

"Honey, why didn't you tell me?"

"I was going to. I meant to tell you that day. That's why I wanted to go to the coffee shop, so we could talk."

Only they'd grabbed her before she could bring it up. Abby remembered everything about that day vividly. She'd been so preoccupied by all she'd had to do that day. Now that she thought back to it, Kenzie had seemed distracted and had tried to start a conversation with her several times but had seemed to lose her nerve each time. Her threats to expose what was happening in their town were the reason they'd had to act and snatch her off the street before she told what she knew about their organization.

Tears filled Abby's eyes. Even when trying to be a good parent, she'd let down her daughter. She pulled Kenzie into a hug. "I won't let you down again."

"You didn't let me down, Aunt Abby. I let *you* down."

"No, you didn't. You could never let me down, Kenzie. I let you down by never telling you the truth about your father."

Her eyes brightened. "You know who my father is?"

She nodded. "Yes, I know. In fact, I know he's out there right now looking for you and now for me. And he won't stop until he finds us."

"He—he's coming for me?"

Abby nodded. "He is."

"Why did he never contact me before?"

Abby took a deep breath and realized that she had a choice to make. She didn't want to turn the girl against her right now, when they were trapped in this dangerous situation and needed to be able to work together. But she couldn't lie either. It was time to finally surrender herself to the truth and trust the people she loved to handle it responsibly. "He didn't know about you, honey. He didn't know he had a daughter until you were gone. I never told him."

Kenzie stared at her, confusion flickering on her face. "What do you mean you never told him? Aunt Abby?"

She sucked in a breath, bracing herself. "I gave birth to you when I was nineteen. I was so young and so driven with my plans for a big career that I knew I couldn't take care of you, so I gave you to my sister and brother-in-law to raise. I know I made the right choice because they were wonderful parents to you and Dustin."

Kenzie sat back on her heels and stared, her mind struggling to put the pieces together. "Aunt Abby, are you trying to tell me that you're…that you're my birth mother?"

Abby nodded. "Yes, I'm your biological mother. Your father, Luke, was my boyfriend at the time. I never told him I was pregnant with you, Kenzie. Once he found out, after you were taken, honey, he's thought of nothing else except finding you. He loves you that much."

She reached out for Kenzie but the girl scooted away, her hands out in a don't-touch-me gesture. Abby lowered her hands. Kenzie's reaction was pretty much what she'd expected. She'd known the news would be a shock to Kenzie. Her guard was up now but Abby wasn't sorry she'd told her. For the first time in her life, she was free from the secrets she'd held on to for so long. Kenzie would hopefully forgive her someday for her deception, and if she didn't, at least Kenzie would still have Dustin and Luke for emotional support.

She glanced around the room they were in. Eight other girls were sitting on mattresses on the floor. Everyone here looked beaten down and weary. There was one window in the room that provided some light, but that she was certain was guarded or nailed shut. The door looked sturdy and was surely locked from the outside. Abby didn't feel good about this. She didn't know how or if they were going to be able to escape. If they didn't, if this was the last opportunity she had to come clean with Kenzie, she was glad she'd taken it.

Abby crawled to her feet, got up and walked to the door. Pain zinged through her head and she was still a bit dizzy from whatever drug they'd given her, but she made it without falling. She couldn't wait for the drugs to wear off. They needed to act now. She tried the handle. Locked. Just as she'd thought. They were prisoners here. But for how long?

Lewis had said in the car that he wasn't going to harm her because the boss wanted to talk to her. In a way, being here was a blessing. She'd found Kenzie and been able to come clean with her. And at some point— hopefully soon—she was finally going to discover who was the brains behind this operation. She was going to be able to look him in the face and confront the man who'd stolen her child.

Lewis's words confirmed that this was a coordinated and organized operation that spanned at least through the county, if not the state or more. She was anxious to see who was behind all of this. Who had placed a target on her and her family and who had put all these girls' families through such pain.

She walked to the window and pulled at it. It wouldn't budge. Just as she'd thought. The windows had been blacked out with paint, but some light filtered in through small chipped places. She tried to look out to get an idea of where they were, but the openings weren't big enough. All she could see were shrubbery and dirt. It didn't feel like they were underground, with the window in the room, but she didn't hear any sounds coming from outside either. Wherever they were, they were being kept isolated. She checked around the edge of the window and felt nails. The windows had been nailed shut to prevent the girls from escaping.

She dug her fingernail into the wooden frame, around the nail. If she could pull the nails loose, maybe they could get free. It would be a start, though what she really wanted was to reach a phone and let Luke know where they were being kept. If she did, she knew that he would come. She had no doubt he was searching for her already. Dustin would have phoned him when he couldn't find her. Her heart wrenched at the idea of him searching the house and ranch for her and never finding her. He must have been so scared. But he would have phoned someone by now, Luke or possibly Janet, who would have phoned Luke. They knew by now that she was missing, and she had no doubt he was searching for her. She'd seen his single-minded determination in hunting for Kenzie. He would do the same for her. Tears pressed against her eyes at the idea that he would move heaven and earth to find them both. He loved them that much. He'd never said it, but she was certain of it. If she had any regrets in all of this, it was that she'd never told him in person how much she loved him. She'd only said it in a stupid voice mail. Now she might not ever get the opportunity to say it to his face. To make certain he understood how important he was to her life. To let him know that she trusted him more than she'd ever trusted anyone before.

And Kenzie. Abby had had her second chance to be a parent to her. Luke deserved the same. It wasn't right that he might never get to know her or that Kenzie would never know just how much her dad loved her. She'd robbed them both of that relationship and she might never have the occasion to correct that.

Her fingernail broke and she gasped at the pain.

Kenzie appeared beside her. "Are you okay? What are you doing?"

"I'm fine. Just trying to pry this nail out of the windowsill. If I can get it loose, we might be able to get out of here and get help."

"I thought you said my father was coming to help us."

"He is, Kenzie. I promise you, he's out there looking for us right now, but we have to help ourselves too. We can't just sit here and be victims. The moment we give up, they've won."

"But—but they're so strong."

Abby turned and gripped her shoulders. "They're only people, Kenzie. They may be physically stronger. They may have weapons. But they're not stronger than you where it really counts. They twist the truth and lie to your face and pretend to offer you the world because what they have to offer you is vile and ugly. Evil always disguises itself in good. They may seem strong, but even that is a lie. They can't break us because we're daughters of the one true Christ and He is stronger than all of them put together."

She glanced around to see the other girls listening to her. She pulled Kenzie to her, then motioned them over as well and said a prayer. "Jesus, we come to You today frightened and weary. We need Your help to fight the evil that has captured us. Send help, Lord, and keep us strong in spirit. In Your precious name we pray. Amen."

On the surface, nothing had changed for them. They were still being held captive and still trapped in this room, but Abby felt something lift from her shoulders and a renewed energy fill the room. Kenzie turned back to trying to dig out the nail from the window and several others hurried to do the same to the other windows.

Abby felt a sense of relief at seeing this. They weren't giving up, which meant they were going to be okay.

Suddenly, the sound of the door unlocking caused them all to gasp and turn. Several girls ran from the windows. Kenzie leaned in close to Abby as the door opened.

Lewis entered the room with several men behind him. He pointed to Abby. "You come with us. It's time."

Abby's heart kicked up a notch. This was the moment she was finally going to discover who was behind this operation.

Kenzie clung to her. "No! Don't go, Aunt Abby. Don't let them take you."

A man walked over and pried Kenzie's arms from Abby, pushed her aside, then pulled Abby toward the door.

Anger pulsed through Abby as he shoved Kenzie away. "Keep your hands off her!"

He reiterated by propelling Abby toward the door. "Get moving."

Abby walked to Lewis and locked eyes with him. "Tell your goons to keep their hands off my niece."

He chuckled. "She'll be fine. You're the one you should be worried about."

She heard Kenzie gasp at that comment

and turned to see tears running down her face. "It'll be okay, Kenzie. I'll be back soon. I promise."

She walked out of the room and Lewis closed and locked the door behind them. He turned to her and smirked. "You really shouldn't make promises you can't keep."

Her heart sank as he walked off. One of his goons grabbed her arm and forced her to follow him. She couldn't help but pray that wasn't the last time she would ever see her daughter.

Luke paced the conference room floor. He couldn't sit. He could hardly even think. His stomach was in knots, his muscles ached with tension, and it felt as if pressure was pounding down on him. Abby was gone, Kenzie was still missing, and he had no idea how to find either of them.

He'd shared Abby's voice mail recording with Caleb, but it had stopped recording before revealing any useful information. What he wouldn't give for a few more seconds of data.

Abby's car had been towed to the police station but so far wasn't offering up any help either. It seemed like Abby's attackers had wiped away their fingerprints before abandoning the vehicle, and any DNA they collected would take time to process. He didn't think Abby had the time to wait for those results. They needed answers now.

An officer walked in and handed Caleb a file. He opened it, then pinched the bridge of his nose. Obviously, not good news.

"What is it?" Luke asked.

"Video surveillance offered us nothing. We can see the cars and the people, but no one is identifiable from the distance and angles."

Luke groaned and pushed a hand through his hair. Frustration rocked him. "What good are video cameras if they can't help identify criminals?"

"Hey, we're a small town. We don't have the resources of the FBI."

"Have them send the video feeds to Amy Pearson at the FBI's Human Trafficking Task Force. Tell her it's from me. Maybe they can enhance the images." It was unlikely but they had to at least try.

What really burned him up was that they had a suspect in the interrogation room who refused to give them any information. Shyla Porter had shut down. She wasn't talking and had lawyered up.

"We need to figure out a way to get her talking," Luke said. He didn't even think about going in there. He was too worked up and would definitely lose his cool if she continued to refuse to help him find the women he loved.

"We can't hold her much longer without charging her. She knows that."

Luke laughed to keep from letting his anger loose. That was about right. Criminals got to hold out, play the system and get away with hurting innocent people, and there was nothing he could do about it.

"What about the surveillance on the garage?" They didn't have the evidence for a warrant to search Buck's Auto Repair Shop, but Luke was certain Pete Lewis was involved, so he'd asked Caleb to place a surveillance team on the shop.

"I spoke with my officers an hour ago. Lewis hasn't been back to the shop since last night. They don't believe he's there. I've ordered another team to switch out with the officers stationed there. Maybe he'll show up now that morning has arrived."

He stared out the window and realized the sun had risen. Abby had been missing for over eight hours. She was probably scared and possibly injured. And she was counting on Luke to do something to save her.

"I'm going to go back through Shyla Porter's financials and phone records. She's got money coming in from somewhere and I want to know where. Maybe I can find something to rattle her so we can get her talking before we have to let her go."

Caleb nodded. "I'll go check in with the forensics team and see if they've found anything else."

He left the room while Luke pulled up a chair and sat down at the conference room table. He grabbed the files they'd printed out on Shyla's bank account. She had funds deposited every few days that they hadn't been able to trace so far and Shyla wasn't offering any explanation for them. Her phone records were clean, but he did notice something odd.

He highlighted several numbers, then pulled up the profiles of the missing girls. Shyla's phone records showed multiple calls to several of the girls' phones after they went missing. Text messages as well as calls lasting several minutes. If the girls hadn't been on the other end of those conversations—and Luke knew they hadn't been—then Shyla had been conversing with whoever had taken their phones. He'd speculated the members of the ring had been using the girls' phones after their abductions. It seemed he was right.

It wasn't much to go on, but it was a detail he could use to try to get her to open up.

Caleb burst back into the room. "I've got something." He held up a crowbar in an evidence bag. Luke recognized it as the one they'd recovered from the scene near Abby's car. "The car was clean but someone forgot to wipe down his crowbar before he left it at the scene. The lab was able to pull a fingerprint." He handed Luke a printout showing a booking photo and information.

The name on the printout was Benny Morris, a career criminal with previous arrests for burglary, strong-arm robbery and assault.

"And look what he lists as his place of employment," Caleb said.

Luke scanned the sheet. Benny was employed by none other than Buck's Auto Repair Shop. "He's one of Lewis's crew?"

"That's what I'm thinking. I've asked for a warrant for his home and place of business."

If they could get Benny talking, they might be able to connect Lewis to the ring and find out who was behind it and where the girls were being held.

Luke suited up for the search, excited to have this new development.

He was one step closer to finding Abby and Kenzie and bringing them home.

Lewis grabbed Abby's arm and dragged her down a long hallway that opened to a sitting room. There was a couch, several foldout chairs and a television. This was obviously where the men who were guarding the girls remained.

They were in a house. She spotted a small kitchen in the corner and saw trees and what looked like a barn in the distance through the window. No other houses or other structures were visible. They must have wanted her to see that and realize how isolated they were, because no one said anything as she stared out the window.

Finally, Lewis pressed her to sit in a chair at the table. Abby glanced around, searching for anything she could grab that would help her to escape or to fight back, but the watchful eyes of her abductors were on her. She counted six men, several of whom she recognized from the auto repair shop. She would never make it out of this farmhouse even if she could grab a weapon. Not that she would even attempt anything like that, of course. She would never abandon Kenzie and the other girls. Even if she just left for long enough to get help and come back, she couldn't risk they would move them and then she would lose Kenzie all over again.

She spotted a man she recognized, even though she hadn't seen him in the garage. "I know you," she told him. "You're the man who abducted Kenzie."

He gave her an amused smile. "You both put up more of a fight than I was expecting." He touched the skin around his eye, which was blue and bruised.

She had the urge to claw his eyes out for starting all of this, but she was smart enough to know now that he'd only been acting on orders. From what Kenzie had shared with her, she'd threatened to expose the organization. They couldn't allow her to do that.

"You gave Adam here a nice shiner that day," Lewis said, laughing.

Adam glared at Lewis, then at her. It was her turn to offer him a smug smile. "Good."

Lewis kept laughing as he walked to the front door, opened it, then stepped outside. "She's ready, Boss."

A shadow crossed the window and a figure appeared in the doorway. Abby held her breath. Her heart was pounding like a jack-hammer. She was finally going to find out who was behind this all.

Lewis reentered the room and a figure moved behind him. Lewis was blocking Abby's line of sight, keeping the new arrival out of her vision until the last possible moment, but when she saw him, she gasped.

In her mind, he'd been a shadowy figure lurking in the background, an out-of-towner who'd come in and set up operations and preyed on people he had no relationship with.

But that wasn't the case. She *knew* this man.

She opened her mouth to speak, but nothing came out. She was stunned.

Trent McDade stood before her. He flashed her his famously friendly, beaming white smile. "Abby, I'm glad to see you've recovered from your ordeal last night."

Anger burst through her shock, giving her back her voice. How dare he speak to her like nothing out of the ordinary had happened? "I don't—I don't understand. Trent? You—you're the one behind all of this? You abducted Kenzie? How could you do that? She and your daughter were best friends."

"It was never my intention to hurt Kenzie. Please, Abby, you know me better than that. She's spent the night at my house. I've driven her and Ashley back and forth to soccer practice. She's practically like my own daughter."

Abby shuddered at the thought. Ashley seemed like a sweet girl and Abby had seen no previous signs that she might be in any kind of danger. Was it possible Trent McDade kept his work and his home life separated? Did his family have any idea what he was involved in? She had a difficult time believing Janet had any knowledge of his involvement in trafficking young girls, but then again, she had a hard time believing Trent was involved, despite the evidence right in front of her.

"Yet you had her abducted and are planning to sell her."

"I'm just the money guy, Abby. I'm a cog in the machine. Sure, I'm the head cog around this county, but I make it a point to stay out of the day-to-day recruiting operations. I have people to do that and, unfortunately, Tiffany felt that Kenzie would be a good fit."

Tiffany. She didn't know whether to be furious at the young woman, or feel sorry for her for being caught up in all of this. In a way, she was a victim too, but she'd targeted Kenzie and that made her the enemy.

"Tiffany felt that Kenzie was so unhappy living with you that she would be glad to be a part of our organization. Unfortunately, Kenzie wouldn't stay in line. We don't usually do out-and-out abductions. We don't usually have to, but Kenzie left us little choice. She threatened our operation…just like you did too. I guess the apple doesn't fall far from the tree, does it?"

She took that statement as a point of pride. "She's a strong girl who's been through a lot. You made a mistake when you tried to pick on her."

His expression hardened. "No, my mistake was not shutting you up earlier. I felt bad for you, and I let my personal feelings for you as my friend affect my judgment. I told Lewis and his people to try to scare you into giving up rather than taking you out right away."

"And how did that work out for you?"

"For us? Not well. For you? Even worse. I'm sorry, Abby, but you forced my hand."

"Did you honestly believe that any number of threats would be enough to make me give up looking for my daughter?" As soon as she said the words, she wished she could bite them back. She hadn't meant to admit her real relationship to him. It just slipped out.

He shrugged, showing not a bit of surprise. "Well, you did give up on her once before. I thought history might repeat itself."

The sting of his comment, and the shock of his knowledge of something so personal, sent her gasping for breath. "How…how did you…?"

"Your sister, God rest her soul, told my wife all about it. How she'd taken in her niece after her mother abandoned her to pursue her dreams of being a newscaster."

Hot tears spilled down Abby's face. He had no right to talk about Danielle that way. She would never have said those things. But then again, how else would he have known?

"My wife also shared with me how overwhelmed you were with being a parent. How you weren't sure you could handle becoming a mother even when you had to step in after Danielle and Matt died."

Abby gasped again. She had had that conversation with Janet, but it had been nearly two years ago, when she'd first had to take guardianship of the kids. She'd poured those thoughts out in a moment of weakness. She would never have actually left Kenzie and

Dustin. She would never have shirked her parental responsibilities...at least, not again.

Now her own words were being used to justify abduction of Kenzie into human trafficking.

"And speaking of your sister..." Trent walked over to a chair, took a seat and crossed his legs. He flashed her that smug look again. "She never liked me, you know. She was a busybody just like you. She kept sticking her nose into things that were none of her business."

Abby didn't like the way this conversation had turned.

"She was too curious for her own good," Trent continued, his voice calm and steady as if he expected her to agree with how utterly logical he was being. "I warned her to back off, but she kept digging into my business. My partners didn't like it, so I had to arrange for a little 'accident.'"

Abby gasped and her heart skipped a beat. She shook her head, refusing to believe what he was implying. She already knew he was a kidnapper and trafficker. Lying wasn't such a stretch. "They died in a car wreck. The police investigated and ruled it an accident. A tire blew out and they flipped over an embankment."

He shrugged. "I might have had a hand in causing that tire to blow out."

She didn't want to believe him, but Lewis laughed and it sent chills through her. They had pushed her car onto the train tracks and burned down her house. Causing a car wreck wasn't out of the realm of possibility. Hot tears pressed against her face as she accepted the truth. "You killed her? You killed them both?"

He shrugged again. "I hoped that would be the end of my trouble with your family, but, unfortunately, you're just as nosy as your sister. I couldn't allow this news story you were trying to get going to find any leverage. It might threaten everything I'd built in this town. Thankfully, you abandoned that, but then your niece/daughter started threatening to tell you about our operation. I knew you'd never give up on a story like that, especially once you learned that she had been a target."

"You destroyed my family and you can sit there and smugly tell me *we* threatened *you*?"

"It's the truth. You and Kenzie threatened my livelihood. You both threatened to expose me. I couldn't allow that. Unfortunately, real estate hasn't been paying out like it used to. I was forced to find other properties to sell."

"These girls are not property."

He stood and turned to Lewis. "How are the plans coming for moving the girls today?"

"I've got one of my men procuring a van to transport them. We'll be on the road in a few hours and to New Orleans by this afternoon."

"Good. My partners are very anxious for us to close up this operation, but I don't want to burn everything down. I want to be able to be back in operation in a few months. Tell Ms. Porter to keep the girls in place in the schools and to keep working on grooming them. I'll be in touch about setting up a new place to keep them."

Abby laughed when she heard him mention Shyla Porter. He turned back to her.

"What's so funny?"

"Shyla Porter? The police are onto her. She's being questioned by them as we speak. The last time I spoke to Luke, he said she was terrified of being arrested. She was telling them everything about your organization. They're probably setting up a raid of this place right now."

His expression hardened and he snapped his fingers. "Check out the perimeter."

Several of the men in the room hurried outside.

He glanced at Abby, then back at Lewis. "And find out where Ms. Porter is right now."

"And what about her?" Lewis asked, motioning toward Abby. He whispered the question, but she heard it.

Trent looked at her. "Put her back in with the others and let her spend a few final hours with her daughter. She's not going to be making the trip to New Orleans."

With those words, Trent McDade walked out of the house. She heard a car door slam, then the squeal of tires as he roared away.

With one command, Trent McDade had sealed her demise.

TEN

Luke led the raid on Buck's Auto Repair Shop, guiding a team of eight men and women into the garage and catching its workers off guard.

To his dismay, Pete Lewis wasn't one of them. He was nowhere in sight.

They arrested all four people present, including Tiffany Bell, whom they caught counting money and sharing photographs of other girls at the school with the men when Luke and Caleb and his team arrived.

He felt satisfied as he walked Benny Morris into the station along with Tiffany Bell and two others. One of these was going to answer his questions about Kenzie's and Abby's whereabouts. They weren't leaving until they did.

He made sure to walk them past Shyla Porter's interrogation room as they went through. He wanted her to know that they were closing in on the trafficking group. The faster they all realized they were in hot water, the more likely they were to start trying to save their own skins.

"Who are we going to start with?" Caleb asked.

Luke knew exactly who the weak link was. "We start with Benny. Not only does he have a slew of outstanding warrants, we have him dead to rights with that fingerprint. We know he was at the scene of an abduction. Either he tells us where the girls are or he goes away for a long time."

He'd already watched Benny's resolve buckling as they arrested him and transported him here. He hadn't said anything incriminating yet, but he was sweating profusely. Luke had him placed into an interrogation room and had the heat turned up. He changed from his tactical gear back into regular clothes so he wouldn't be too intimidating. As he buttoned up his shirt, he was already replaying in his head the strategy he would take. He'd assure Benny that what he was offering him was a second chance and remind him that those didn't come along very often.

He stopped, struck by the realization that he'd been fighting against that very thing.

He'd been given a second chance to be a dad, a second chance with Abby, even a second chance to live at the ranch.

Why had he been fighting so hard against it all, then? Holding on to his anger and bitterness and looking for any excuse to push away everything he'd ever wished for.

Abby had been right about everything.

He pulled out his cell phone and listened to her voice mail again, his heart melting at hearing her say she loved him. She was everything he'd ever wanted for as long as he could remember. She might not have made the perfect choices, but neither had he. He was ready to enjoy life, ready to put aside his anger and resentment and just be happy for once.

That Bible verse from Proverbs 10:12 that Ed had posted on the wall of the barn came back to him. *Hatred stirreth up strifes: but love covereth all sins*. Luke had spent so many years clinging on to his anger and hatred that it had bled into all areas of his life. Every offense against him had been nursed into a grudge and he was tired of living this way. For the first time, he realized that love really could cover all sins. He didn't have to continue to fight to keep hold of his anger at

Abby's betrayal. He could instead allow his love for her to grow and wipe it away...the same way Jesus's love for him could wipe away all his sins.

He blew out a breath and realized the truth. He was ready to surrender. Abby hadn't been the only one with control issues. He needed to let go too and trust that God, who had brought him to within arm's length of everything he'd ever wanted, had a plan for his life.

I'm done fighting, God. I'm trusting in Your plan.

The locker room door opened and Caleb stood there. "Benny's ready. Do you want me to question him?"

Luke shook his head, then stood. "No, I'll do it." This suspect was going to lead him to his family and he was going to bring them home.

They were going to have their promised second chance.

Lewis grabbed Abby's arm and dragged her back to the locked room. He opened the door, then tossed her inside. She heard the clang of the lock as it was reengaged. The door was solid and steel, probably installed just to keep them inside.

They weren't getting out that way.

Kenzie ran to her and threw her arms around her. Abby hugged her back but her focus now was on getting all of them out of here. Trent had made it clear the girls were being moved, and if they were, it seemed highly likely that no one would ever find them. Not to mention he'd also basically given Lewis orders to end Abby's life before they left.

Their time was limited.

"Look, Abby, we got one out." Kenzie held a long rusty nail in her hand. "We've been using it to pull the others out too."

Hope felt good. "Nice work. Let's get finished before they return. I heard them say that they're moving everyone in a few hours. We have to get free from this room before that happens."

She hurried to the window to help the girls. They were able to pull out three nails from the sill, a hard-earned victory. Abby pushed at the window. It still didn't budge, but these old windows were probably also warped and painted shut. She hit the sill in several places, then pushed again. Kenzie and another girl joined her on either side and pushed too. Finally, she felt the window give. Relief swept through her. She was going to be able to get these girls to safety.

She continued pushing at the window until it was up enough for the girls to crawl through.

"I'm staying with you," Kenzie said, grabbing her arm.

"I'm going. I'll just be the last one out."

"Then I'll be the next-to-the-last one. No more splitting up, remember?"

She was glad Kenzie didn't want to leave her side, but this was one instance where she wished she would. She didn't know how much time they would have before Lewis or one of the others came back, and she wanted Kenzie as far away from this room as possible when that happened. But she didn't have time to argue. She pressed the other girls to go first, and they did, crawling out one by one. She heard the sounds of their footsteps as they took off running.

Finally, it was just Kenzie. "Go," Abby told her. "Hurry."

Kenzie climbed through the opening and Abby quickly followed her. She didn't relax even as her feet hit dirt. They weren't out of the woods yet. The rest of the girls had sprinted away and, thankfully, it didn't seem like anyone had been alerted to their escape yet. No one was chasing them. However, as

Abby glanced around and realized they were at the old Ruston Farm, her hopes sank. This place was very far off the beaten path and extremely isolated, which meant they would have a long way to go before reaching someone who could help. All while being hunted by the men currently inside the house.

She glanced back at the building. She needed to get back in there and find a phone to call Luke for help. She glanced at the vehicles parked in front of the house and wondered if one of them had a cell phone...or a set of keys. She wasn't holding her breath that these guys were reckless enough to leave their keys in the ignition, but she could hope, couldn't she?

Why hadn't she ever learned to hot-wire a car?

Kenzie stayed by her side as they moved toward the vehicles. She kept one eye on the house as they crouched down and sneaked slowly toward the parked cars, hoping to remain unseen. Carefully, she opened one of the doors and leaned inside, searching for a cell phone or keys. She couldn't find either one.

She moved to the next car, repeating the process with the same results. By the fourth car, she was beginning to feel this was a fool's errand—however, when she opened the door, her heart skipped a beat. Someone's cell phone sat in the cup holder. She grabbed it and pressed the button. A screen came up asking for a passcode. She didn't have one, but she also knew she didn't need one in order to make emergency calls. All phones could call 911.

She pressed the numbers. She didn't even realize she was holding her breath until she heard the 911 dispatch answer, asking for her emergency.

Success!

"My name is Abby Mitchell. I've been kidnapped by a human trafficking ring. They're holding me and several teenage girls hostage at the old Ruston Farm. Please tell police chief Harmon and his cousin FBI agent Luke Harmon."

The woman started asking a series of questions, which Abby answered until she glanced up and heard a noise.

"Hey, what are you doing?" The shout came from the porch.

"Abby, run!" Kenzie yelled, pulling at her shirt.

The 911 operator was still talking to her, but Abby bolted, pushing Kenzie to go faster.

The other girls were already out of sight, which left her and Kenzie as the targets.

"Abby, let's go!" Kenzie screamed.

She heard yelling from inside the house. They must have discovered the room was empty. Footsteps on the porch told her multiple people were now coming after them.

She did a quick survey of where they were. Aside from the house and cars, there was a large barn to one side, a patch of woods to the other and a dirt path that led to the main road.

Hiding in the woods would be their best chance of staying alive until Luke and the police arrived to rescue them…if they made it in time.

Luke walked into the interview room, dropped the file and a paper sack on the table and took a moment to roll up his sleeves. He didn't want to go at Benny full force—at least, not right away. His plan was to slow-walk him into spilling everything he knew about the trafficking ring. It would require patience and time…time that they really didn't have. Luke couldn't think about that. He had to rely on the process and pray that Benny really was the weak link in the organization.

Finally, Luke sat down and opened the file. Sweat was pouring off Benny and he looked ready to crack. Good. He deserved all the torment he got for his part in this. Luke did his best to push the image from his mind of this giant man dragging Abby from her car and possibly threatening her with a crowbar. He had to remain calm or he could blow this opportunity.

Luke stared at Benny's police record, then whistled. "Looks like you've had a few run-ins with the law, Benny. Assault, burglary, strong-arm robbery."

He shrugged and put up a false bravado. "Hardly any of those charges stuck."

Luke saw he was right. Most of the charges had either been pleaded down to misdemeanors or dropped altogether when the victims and witnesses recanted their stories. He was sure intimidation or outright threats against them had nothing to do with it.

"And we weren't doing anything when you barged in and arrested us. You've got nothing to keep me here."

"Actually, you've got three open warrants, Benny. Two for assault and one for receiving stolen property."

"They won't hold up either." He was trying

to play it cool, but Luke could see he wasn't nearly as confident as he wanted Luke to believe.

"Maybe not, but it means I can hold you. Besides, I'm pretty sure I have something that's going to stick." Benny watched him with curious eyes as Luke opened the bag and pulled out an evidence bag containing the crowbar they'd found at the scene of Abby's abduction. He plopped it down on the table.

Benny sighed and wiped sweat from his forehead.

"Recognize this?"

His expression said he did. "Never seen it before."

"That's odd because it's got your fingerprints all over it. Guess where we found it? At the scene of an abduction. This crowbar places you at that scene, Benny. That means you're going down for kidnapping. So while you might not be worried about the rest of these charges, you should be worried about this one, because it carries a life sentence."

Benny wiped his head again. Luke could tell he was rattled.

"You know the drill, Benny. You help yourself by telling me what I want to know. Where are the girls being kept? And who's behind this trafficking ring? Answer those questions for me and we can make a deal."

Benny leaned against the table, pondering his decision. Finally, he gave a resigned sigh and nodded. "Okay. I'll tell what you want to know."

"Who's in charge?"

"The head dude is some real-estate guy named Trent McDade. He has access to a lot of empty homes. Ones that are up for sale or foreclosed. He uses them to house the girls."

Luke recognized the name McDade. Abby's neighbor and the father of Kenzie's lifelong best friend. He'd played the caring father and good friend when they'd gone to interview Ashley about Kenzie's whereabouts. And his wife had watched Dustin on multiple occasions. Did she know what her husband had been up to?

"Why did you abduct Abby?"

"McDade said she was becoming a problem. They thought with her gone, no one else would be looking for the girl."

Unfortunately for them all, they didn't know about Kenzie's FBI father, who would never give up searching for her.

His jaw tightened. He couldn't wait to get his hands on this guy and make sure he paid for the torment he'd put them all through. "So you and Lewis captured Abby. What did you do with her?"

"We cornered her, busted in the window on her car and drugged her. I heard Lewis say that McDade wanted to confront her before he killed her. I helped load her into Lewis's car, but then I went home. I have no idea where he took her or what happened to her."

That meant that Trent McDade knew her whereabouts. Luke turned and glanced at the two-way mirror. Caleb would be there watching and would have heard Benny's explanation. If Luke knew his cousin, he was already starting the process of tracking down McDade's location.

Normally, Luke would have left the room to make sure it was done, but he had another pressing issue to deal with first. If McDade knew he was cornered, he might move the girls. They needed to know their location and Benny was the one talking.

"What about the girls? Where are they being housed now?"

"The last I knew, the girls are being held at the old Ruston Farm. It's been in foreclosure for years and McDade is handling the sale. Only, he's not actually looking for buyers.

He's been using that place along with a few others, moving the girls around. After you all located the factory, they moved them there." He shrugged. "At least, that's what Lewis told me. I'm not part of this organization. I only do work when Lewis pays me to."

Luke stood. "Then Lewis has pulled you into a mess, Benny. But you did the right thing by cooperating with us. Once we find the girls and Abby, I'll talk to the prosecutor on your behalf."

He took the file and the crowbar and walked out. Benny would still be facing charges, but he was a small fish. Luke wanted the big catch. The man who'd started this. Trent McDade.

Caleb approached him. "We called Mc-Dade's home and office. He's not at either, but I'm sending patrols to both regardless. I've got warrants coming to search both and I've put a BOLO out on his car. I'm also requesting his financials and phone records."

His cousin was efficient and Luke was appreciative. But now they had a choice to make. "Benny says the girls are being held at the old Ruston Farm."

"I know the place. It's isolated. No one would hear or see anyone coming or going."

He didn't like the idea of having to choose between going after either Abby or Kenzie, but he knew where Kenzie was most likely to be found and Abby's location wasn't certain. McDade could have her in any of the empty homes and businesses Benny had referred to. Besides, Abby would want him to make certain Kenzie was rescued first. "Let's head to the farm. Do you have someone who can go to McDade's office and find out all the empty buildings he has access to? He might have taken Abby to one of them."

"I'll take care of it."

Luke headed to the locker room to suit up again for a raid on the farm. He prayed they wouldn't be too late. McDade had to know by now that several of his people were in custody. He might decide to move the girls right away, and if he did, Luke might lose his last chance at finding his daughter.

Lord, please keep her and Abby safe until I can get to them.

Abby followed Kenzie into a wooded area and together they crouched down behind a tree as several men entered the woods behind them, guns drawn and ready to use. She hugged Kenzie to her. They might not want to kill their merchandise, but they wouldn't let them get away either.

She felt Kenzie's pulse racing and did her best to calm her. "It's okay," she assured her. "Help is coming." She reached for the phone in her pocket, only to find it gone. Panic struck her. She must have dropped it as she'd run.

She glanced around for it and spotted something on the ground near the edge of the tree line. That had to be the phone. If she could reach it, she could help the police find them.

"Stay here and be quiet," she told Kenzie. "I'll be right back."

"Don't leave me." The girl grabbed her arm and clung to her.

"I need to go get the phone. Keep still and you'll be safe."

She unclenched Kenzie's hand from her arm, then stood. She glanced around. No one was in sight. This was her chance to retrieve the phone. She'd already told the dispatcher where they were, but the temptation to hear the sound of someone else's voice and to know help was on the way was undeniable. She hurried through the bushes and branches, then darted toward the phone.

Someone grabbed her from behind as she

reached down for it. She screamed and spun around, trying to kick and scratch herself free. She felt her elbow hit its mark and the grip around her loosened. She ran back toward the barn since her assailant was now blocking her path. She wouldn't lead him back to Kenzie.

She turned and realized her pursuer was none other than Trent. He must have come back, alerted by his men that their inventory had escaped.

"You won't get away with this, Abby," he hollered.

She turned and ran into the barn. Maybe she could find something inside that she could use to fight back against him. She spotted a shovel in the corner and ran to it, but Trent was on top of her before she could put her hands on it.

He seized her. She kicked at him and struggled, but this time he managed to pin her arms and legs. "Calm down. You won't get away this time." His voice had lost its charming, friendly, neighborly veneer. It seemed this wasn't just a business anymore. It was personal. "I said calm down." He smacked her, sending her to the ground as pain burst from her face.

She held her cheek, then stared up at him.

"Do you think you've won, Abby? You haven't. My men will find the girls and bring them back. Even your precious Kenzie. You'll watch the vans take them away—and then I'll kill you. There's no escape."

She swallowed hard, realizing that he might be right. This might very well be the end for her. She couldn't imagine not getting to say goodbye to Luke. Never getting the chance to tell him how much she loved him. Because she did love him. She'd fallen completely in love with him all over again.

The sound of sirens in the distance sent relief flooding through her. Luke had gotten the message. They were saved.

Trent walked to the barn door and glanced out. She couldn't see his face, but his shoulders slumped at what he saw. She could hear the cars with sirens pulling into the entrance of the farm.

Trent and his men were as good as trapped.

She reached for the shovel, closing her hand around it as he turned back to her. She swung it hard, sending him to his knees. She ran for the door, the idea of falling into Luke's waiting arms more appealing than she could say.

A shot sounded and something stung at her side.

She stopped and spun around. Trent was on the ground, gun raised. She looked down and saw blood blooming on her shirt.

He'd shot her.

Voices from outside filtered in. Shouting and screaming about gunfire coming from the barn. She could barely hear them over the pounding of her own pulse.

She'd been shot.

Trent grabbed her, pulling her against him as he raised the gun toward the barn door, where the voices were getting louder and louder.

He was going to use her as a shield to protect himself, then probably kill her...assuming she didn't die from her current wound.

She heard his heart pounding and sweat was pouring off him. "I won't go," he whispered. "I won't go to prison."

Dread filled her. When those doors opened, someone was going to die.

It would probably be her.

Luke turned his SUV into the Ruston Farm and screeched to a halt. Dispatch had routed a call they'd recorded from Abby saying she was at the farm. Hearing her terrified voice had shaken him, but at least he knew where she was and that she was alive for the moment.

He jumped from the SUV, gun at the ready. Men were scattering and he heard the cries of female voices coming from the woods. "Spread your men out," he shouted to Caleb. "Find the girls and find Lewis."

He wasn't sure who he wanted to capture more—Lewis or McDade.

He didn't bother with the woods. He ran toward the house. If McDade was here, he would be in the building, not out chasing girls through the brush. The scene was chaotic and not what he'd expected when they'd headed here. Abby's call had alerted them that the girls, and she, had escaped. That meant the guards would be occupied trying to retrieve them. Their arrival would have taken them by surprise and they would now be scrambling.

Luke heard commotion from behind him but he blocked it out as he approached the cars. He spotted one he recognized from the BOLO as belonging to McDade.

He was here.

Luke stepped onto the porch and pushed open the front door of the farmhouse. The living area was empty. He checked the other rooms, including one with a steel door and a lot of locks. Obviously where they'd kept the girls. It looked like they'd managed to get out through a window.

He clicked on his mic to speak to his team. "The house is clear."

Caleb's voice responded. "We've captured several of the guards, including Lewis."

Luke breathed a sigh of relief. That was good news.

"He claims he saw McDade run into the barn after Abby. Then he heard a gunshot," Caleb continued. "I'm heading there now."

Luke's heart stopped at that revelation. "I'll meet you there."

He ran from the house. The old barn was set to the side. He hadn't heard a gunshot, so if someone was hurt in there, it had happened before they'd arrived. And if Abby hadn't come out after hearing them approach…well, it wasn't good.

His pulse raced as he approached the barn, his mind spinning at what he might find inside.

Caleb rushed to him. "So far, my team has captured six men and found four of the girls. They're still searching the woods for the rest. Any signs of Kenzie or Abby?"

"Not yet. McDade either, but that's his car parked by the house," Luke told him.

Caleb looked at the barn and his jaw tensed. "I'll go around back. I'll let you know when I'm in position."

Luke nodded, but every second it took Caleb to get into position seemed like an eternity. "I'm here," came the call finally.

Luke raised his weapon, braced himself, then approached the barn. He pulled open the door. His heart skipped a beat when he saw McDade holding Abby like a shield with a gun to her head.

He'd found her and, just as he'd feared, she was in peril.

"Let her go," he demanded, aiming his gun at McDade's head. He was hiding behind Abby, which made a clean shot dangerous.

"Get back," McDade demanded, pressing the gun against her. "I'll kill her."

"You're surrounded, Trent. What do you think you're going to do?"

"We're going to walk to my car and leave. Once I'm gone, I'll leave her on the side of the road."

"That's never going to happen." Like he would trust Trent to keep his word, especially when it came to the welfare of a woman he'd been trying to kill all week.

He responded by pressing the gun harder,

causing Abby to cry out. "I said get back or I'll shoot her."

Luke took his eyes off McDade for a moment to look at Abby. She was pale and frightened and he noticed blood on her shirt. She was holding her stomach and red was pooling around her fingers. She'd been shot already.

They needed to end this quickly.

"We're at the back of the barn," Caleb said through his earpiece. A moment later, a team of men appeared behind Trent. "You're surrounded," he told Trent. "There's nowhere to go. Let the lady go."

Instead of giving in, Trent doubled down. "I said get back or I'll kill her. I'll do it." He pulled her into a stall so his back was against a wall. There was no way to escape but he was also no longer exposed from behind.

"Do you have a shot?" Caleb asked him.

Luke shook his head. The target was too narrow. He couldn't risk Abby being hit. But he also knew she was bleeding and needed help. If he hesitated too long, she could bleed out. He needed to take the risk.

Flashbacks of his showdown on his last mission flowed through him. He'd hesitated then with disastrous consequences. Shelton had killed Michelle because Luke had been too worried about the consequences to fire. He couldn't take the chance of the same thing happening to Abby.

He had to risk it.

He stared into Trent's wild eyes. He had no intention of going quietly. They were not able to negotiate their way out of this, and even if they could, Abby might not have that kind of time. Trent would do serious damage on his way down.

He glanced at Abby. She seemed to sense what he was thinking and nodded her understanding, indicating that she would get herself out of the way as best she could.

God, please make my aim straight.

"Trent, put the gun down and let Abby go. Let's end this." One last chance to do the right thing. Luke prayed he would take it.

He knew Trent wouldn't the moment his eyes squinted and his finger pressed on the trigger.

Luke fired, hitting his mark. Trent went down, pulling Abby down with him.

Luke hurried toward them, keeping his weapon trained on Trent, but it was obvious to him once he saw him that he wasn't getting back up.

Trent McDade was dead.

He took the gun from the dead man's hand, then knelt beside Abby. She was breathing heavily and her face was paler than he'd ever seen it.

"Did I get you?"

She shook her head. "No, you didn't hit me."

The rest of the team hurried into the barn as he moved her hand away to examine her wound. "What happened?"

"He—he shot me as I was trying to escape."

Anger filled him. "We need an ambulance," he called to whoever would listen. "Hang on, Abby. Help is on the way."

She touched his arm. "The girls. Kenzie. Are they okay?"

"I'm not sure about Kenzie, but I know Caleb's men found some girls hiding in the woods. You got them out, Abby. You did a good thing."

She laid her head back on the hay as all her energy seemed to flow out of her. "I knew you'd come," she told him. "I knew you were looking for us. I never doubted that."

"You never have to. I'll always be here for you. I love you, Abby."

She smiled, but her eyelids were fluttering, and he sensed she was fighting back unconsciousness. The sounds of the ambulance sirens were music to his ears.

"Help is on the way, Abby. Hang on. Don't you leave me again."

She shook her head. "I won't." She reached up to touch his face. "I want us to be a family."

He nodded but felt tears flooding his eyes. "I want that too."

Her hand fell away as she closed her eyes and leaned back. He caught it and held it. The paramedics rushed inside and he stepped away from her to let them work. "She has a gunshot on her right lower abdomen. She's lost a lot of blood."

They quickly stabilized her, then loaded her onto a gurney and wheeled her out to the waiting ambulance.

As the doors closed, a girl ran toward the ambulance. "Aunt Abby!"

Luke grabbed her arm as the ambulance pulled away. "She's okay. She was shot, but they're taking her to the hospital."

She turned to look up at him and all the breath in his body seemed to leave him. The blond hair and heart-shaped face could have been Abby twenty years ago. Except for the eyes. Those were his eyes.

"Are you Kenzie?"

She nodded.

"My name is Luke Harmon. I'm a friend of Abby's."

Her eyes widened as she stared up at him. "You're him. You're my father."

He suddenly felt put on the spot. She knew who he was? Abby must have told her. "I am."

She stared up at him, her blue eyes seeming to quiz him. Then she suddenly pressed herself against him and circled his waist with her arms.

His daughter was hugging him. He embraced her, his heart kicking up a beat at the swelling of love that suddenly rushed through him.

He was hugging his daughter.

He stroked her hair and soaked in the feeling of her. *Thank You, God, for allowing me this precious moment.* He'd been so worried he might never get to meet her.

His voice cracked with emotion as he spoke to her. "It's so nice to meet you, Kenzie."

She smiled. "You too." Then her eyes clouded up and she frowned. "Aunt Abby."

"I'll take you to the hospital to see how she is."

She nodded, then followed him to his SUV. He stopped before starting the engine and turned to Kenzie.

"I guess Abby told you about me? What did she say?"

Kenzie stared up at him. "She told me you would never stop looking for us." She gave him a smile. "And she was right. You didn't stop looking for me."

She'd told him the same thing, but to hear her words from Kenzie made his heart swell. She'd trusted him to find her. She'd known he wouldn't stop looking. Her faith in him meant the world.

He drove to the hospital and waited for information about Abby. An hour later, the doors opened and Caleb entered with Dustin behind him.

"Kenzie!" Dustin ran and pulled his sister into a hug. She hugged him back tightly. "I thought I might not see you again. I'm so glad you're okay."

"Me too, Dustin. I'm sorry I was away so long."

Dustin glanced at Luke. "Where's Aunt Abby? Is she okay?"

Kenzie drew him to her. "She's going to be fine."

"Yes, she is," Luke told him. "She was shot, but the doctors say she's going to be fine."

A nurse appeared at the door and called

to Luke. "The surgery went well and she's awake and in recovery. You can see her now."

He led the kids back to her hospital room and nearly gasped when he spotted Abby lying in the bed. She looked frail and weak, but she perked up when she saw the kids. Kenzie ran to her and hugged her, and Dustin followed suit.

"I'm okay," she assured them. She glanced at Kenzie. "What about you? How are you?"

"I'm fine," the girl insisted. "I will be fine."

Abby turned to him and Luke pulled a chair to the edge of the bed and held her hand. "The doctor said the bullet didn't do any major damage. They were able to remove it with no problem. You're going to be up and around soon."

She entangled her fingers in his. "Thanks to you. I knew you would come for me."

"Always." He stroked her face. "I don't ever want to be without you again, Abby. Maybe I shouldn't do this in front of the kids and maybe I should wait until you're on your feet again and out of the hospital, but I don't want to waste another day. I want us to be a family. All of us. Will you marry me?"

"Does that mean you're staying in Jessup?"

He smiled. "God has put everything I love here. Why would I ever leave?"

Tears filled her eyes and she bit her lip to hold back her emotions. "God?" Her voice was so full of hope that he laughed to keep from crying.

He nodded, then kissed her hand. "Yes. I've found more in this town than I ever knew I wanted. You, the kids, the ranch and even my faith."

"I'm so glad we've both stopped running." She stroked his cheek. "Then yes, Luke Harmon, I will marry you. I love you."

Kenzie squealed and smiled at them, then leaned her head on her brother's shoulder. Dustin grinned at them both.

Abby reached for their hands, and Kenzie and Dustin rushed to her and Luke. They were all together again, and this time, nothing would separate them.

EPILOGUE

Abby grabbed a handful of drinks and tucked them in a cooling bag along with the sandwiches she'd made, then carried them outside. They'd planned a picnic by the lake for the family to celebrate their six months together.

She stared at the wedding ring on her finger as the sounds of Dustin and Luke laughing floated through the window. They'd had a small wedding, not wanting to wait long enough to plan a larger one, and her friends and coworkers had been understanding. They had only Kenzie, Dustin and Caleb, Ed and Hannah as witnesses. After the wedding, they made Harmon Ranch their permanent home. Caleb had been thrilled that Luke was staying in town and claiming his quarter of the ranch, and the house was big enough that they had plenty of privacy even with Caleb still living there too. She and Luke had already spent too much time apart, and neither of them had wanted to wait another day to be together.

Luke's FBI hearing had cleared him of any wrongdoing in Michelle Simmons's death, but he'd decided to retire anyway, not wanting to uproot his new family. Abby was delighted to see that he was learning to love life on the ranch and replacing the old, bitter memories with newer, happy ones.

Trent McDade and his cohorts were all awaiting trial on kidnapping, murder and trafficking charges, while his wife and daughter had left town humiliated by the scandal that erupted after his arrest. However, taking down Trent's operation had helped Luke's FBI colleagues infiltrate several other rings operating around the country.

Abby stepped outside and saw Dustin and Luke saddling up the horses while Kenzie sat in the dirt holding a baby goat. The smile of contentment on her face was soothing and healing.

Luke walked over to her and grabbed the cooler before securing it on the horse. He pulled her to him. "How is she doing?"

She glanced at Kenzie. She'd been through an ordeal, but she'd come out stronger the other side. They all had. "She's going to be fine," Abby told him. "We all are." She turned toward the fence. "Kenzie, put the baby goat down," Abby called. "We're ready to go."

Kenzie hopped up and returned the goat to its pen before joining them. Luke grabbed the horses' reins and held them as they walked toward the lake, Kenzie beside her while Dustin walked next to Luke.

Luke took her hand and kissed it, then leaned over and claimed her lips too. She soaked in the feeling of him, still filled with joy that she'd reached this point of happiness in her life.

She'd made so many mistakes and wrong choices that it still amazed her that God had fixed them all. They were all together again. She and Luke, Kenzie and Dustin. They were a family now and Abby was so grateful for the second chance God had given her.

He'd given them all a second chance at being a family.

* * * * *

Dear Readers,

The start of a brand-new series is always exciting! I look forward to getting to know these new characters, new settings and new romances. Thank you for joining me on this new journey. I hope you enjoyed getting to know Luke, Abby, Kenzie and Dustin as much as I did. I hope you'll join me for the next book in the series.

I love to hear from my readers! Please keep in touch. You can reach me online at my website, www.virginiavaughanonline.com, or follow me on Facebook at www.Facebook.com/ginvaughanbooks.

Blessings!
Virginia

Get 4 FREE REWARDS!

We'll send you 2 FREE Books plus 2 FREE Mystery Gifts.

FREE Value Over **$20**

Both the **Love Inspired**® and **Love Inspired**® Suspense series feature compelling novels filled with inspirational romance, faith, forgiveness and hope.

YES! Please send me 2 FREE novels from the Love Inspired or Love Inspired Suspense series and my 2 FREE gifts (gifts are worth about $10 retail). After receiving them, if I don't wish to receive any more books, I can return the shipping statement marked "cancel." If I don't cancel, I will receive 6 brand-new Love Inspired Larger-Print books or Love Inspired Suspense Larger-Print books every month and be billed just $6.49 each in the U.S. or $6.74 each in Canada. That is a savings of at least 16% off the cover price. It's quite a bargain! Shipping and handling is just 50¢ per book in the U.S. and $1.25 per book in Canada.* I understand that accepting the 2 free books and gifts places me under no obligation to buy anything. I can always return a shipment and cancel at any time by calling the number below. The free books and gifts are mine to keep no matter what I decide.

Choose one: ☐ **Love Inspired**
Larger-Print
(122/322 IDN GRHK)

☐ **Love Inspired Suspense**
Larger-Print
(107/307 IDN GRHK)

Name (please print)

Address   Apt. #

City   State/Province   Zip/Postal Code

Email: Please check this box ☐ if you would like to receive newsletters and promotional emails from Harlequin Enterprises ULC and its affiliates. You can unsubscribe anytime.

Mail to the Harlequin Reader Service:
IN U.S.A.: P.O. Box 1341, Buffalo, NY 14240-8531
IN CANADA: P.O. Box 603, Fort Erie, Ontario L2A 5X3

Want to try 2 free books from another series? Call 1-800-873-8635 or visit www.ReaderService.com.

*Terms and prices subject to change without notice. Prices do not include sales taxes, which will be charged (if applicable) based on your state or country of residence. Canadian residents will be charged applicable taxes. Offer not valid in Quebec. This offer is limited to one order per household. Books received may not be as shown. Not valid for current subscribers to the Love Inspired or Love Inspired Suspense series. All orders subject to approval. Credit or debit balances in a customer's account(s) may be offset by any other outstanding balance owed by or to the customer. Please allow 4 to 6 weeks for delivery. Offer available while quantities last.

Your Privacy—Your information is being collected by Harlequin Enterprises ULC, operating as Harlequin Reader Service. For a complete summary of the information we collect, how we use this information and to whom it is disclosed, please visit our privacy notice located at corporate.harlequin.com/privacy-notice. From time to time we may also exchange your personal information with reputable third parties. If you wish to opt out of this sharing of your personal information, please visit readerservice.com/consumerschoice or call 1-800-873-8635. **Notice to California Residents**—Under California law, you have specific rights to control and access your data. For more information on these rights and how to exercise them, visit corporate.harlequin.com/california-privacy.

LIRLIS22R3

Get 4 FREE REWARDS!

We'll send you 2 FREE Books plus 2 FREE Mystery Gifts.

FREE
Value Over
$20

Both the **Harlequin® Special Edition** and **Harlequin® Heartwarming™** series feature compelling novels filled with stories of love and strength where the bonds of friendship, family and community unite.

YES! Please send me 2 FREE novels from the Harlequin Special Edition or Harlequin Heartwarming series and my 2 FREE gifts (gifts are worth about $10 retail). After receiving them, if I don't wish to receive any more books, I can return the shipping statement marked "cancel." If I don't cancel, I will receive 6 brand-new Harlequin Special Edition books every month and be billed just $5.49 each in the U.S. or $6.24 each in Canada, a savings of at least 12% off the cover price, or 4 brand-new Harlequin Heartwarming Larger-Print books every month and be billed just $6.24 each in the U.S. or $6.74 each in Canada, a savings of at least 19% off the cover price. It's quite a bargain! Shipping and handling is just 50¢ per book in the U.S. and $1.25 per book in Canada.* I understand that accepting the 2 free books and gifts places me under no obligation to buy anything. I can always return a shipment and cancel at any time by calling the number below. The free books and gifts are mine to keep no matter what I decide.

Choose one: ☐ **Harlequin Special Edition**
(235/335 HDN GRJV)
☐ **Harlequin Heartwarming Larger-Print**
(161/361 HDN GRJV)

_____
Name (please print)

_____
Address   Apt. #

_____
City   State/Province   Zip/Postal Code

Email: Please check this box ☐ if you would like to receive newsletters and promotional emails from Harlequin Enterprises ULC and its affiliates. You can unsubscribe anytime.

Mail to the **Harlequin Reader Service:**
IN U.S.A.: P.O. Box 1341, Buffalo, NY 14240-8531
IN CANADA: P.O. Box 603, Fort Erie, Ontario L2A 5X3

Want to try 2 free books from another series! Call 1-800-873-8635 or visit www.ReaderService.com.

*Terms and prices subject to change without notice. Prices do not include sales taxes, which will be charged (if applicable) based on your state or country of residence. Canadian residents will be charged applicable taxes. Offer not valid in Quebec. This offer is limited to one order per household. Books received may not be as shown. Not valid for current subscribers to the Harlequin Special Edition or Harlequin Heartwarming series. All orders subject to approval. Credit or debit balances in a customer's account(s) may be offset by any other outstanding balance owed by or to the customer. Please allow 4 to 6 weeks for delivery. Offer available while quantities last.

Your Privacy—Your information is being collected by Harlequin Enterprises ULC, operating as Harlequin Reader Service. For a complete summary of the information we collect, how we use this information and to whom it is disclosed, please visit our privacy notice located at corporate.harlequin.com/privacy-notice. From time to time we may also exchange your personal information with reputable third parties. If you wish to opt out of this sharing of your personal information, please visit readerservice.com/consumerschoice or call 1-800-873-8635. **Notice to California Residents**—Under California law, you have specific rights to control and access your data. For more information on these rights and how to exercise them, visit corporate.harlequin.com/california-privacy.

HSEHW22R3

THE 2022 LOVE INSPIRED CHRISTMAS COLLECTION

Buy 3 and get 1 FREE!

May all that is beautiful, meaningful and brings you joy be yours this holiday season...including this fun-filled collection featuring 24 Christmas stories. From tender holiday romances to Christmas Eve suspense, this collection has it all.

YES! Please send me the **2022 LOVE INSPIRED CHRISTMAS COLLECTION** in Larger Print! This collection begins with ONE FREE book and 2 FREE gifts in the first shipment. Along with my FREE book, I'll get another 3 Larger Print books! If I do not cancel, I will continue to receive four books a month for five more months. Each shipment will contain another FREE gift. I'll pay just $23.97 U.S./$26.97 CAN., plus $1.99 U.S./$4.99 CAN. for shipping and handling per shipment.* I understand that accepting the free books and gifts places me under no obligation to buy anything. I can always return a shipment and cancel at any time. My free books and gifts are mine to keep no matter what I decide.

☐ 298 HCK 0958   ☐ 498 HCK 0958

Name (please print)

Address   Apt. #

City   State/Province   Zip/Postal Code

Mail to the Harlequin Reader Service:
IN U.S.A.: P.O. Box 1341, Buffalo, NY 14240-8531
IN CANADA: P.O. Box 603, Fort Erie, ON L2A 5X3

---

*Terms and prices subject to change without notice. Prices do not include sales taxes, which will be charged (if applicable) based on your state or country of residence. Canadian residents will be charged applicable taxes. Offer not valid in Quebec. All orders subject to approval. Credit or debit balances in a customer's account(s) may be offset by any other outstanding balance owed by or to the customer. Please allow 3 to 4 weeks for delivery. Offer available while quantities last. © 2022 Harlequin Enterprises ULC. ® and ™ are trademarks owned by Harlequin Enterprises ULC.

Your Privacy—Your information is being collected by Harlequin Enterprises ULC, operating as Harlequin Reader Service. To see how we collect and use this information visit https://corporate.harlequin.com/privacy-notice. From time to time we may also exchange your personal information with reputable third parties. If you wish to opt out of this sharing of your personal information, please visit www.readerservice.com/consumerschoice or call 1-800-873-8635. Notice to California Residents—Under California law, you have specific rights to control and access your data. For more information visit https://corporate.harlequin.com/california-privacy.